"How serious is it?" Tara half whispered

"Luckily for you it's more of a warning than anything else." Ryan's hard eyes blazed with fury. "But if you go on having assignations with Moncrieff, who's just about the biggest shark ever to swim out of Australian waters, you'll probably kill your father!"

"If I go . . ." The implication of his words suddenly clicked in her brain. Fury, as great as his, fueled by her worry, swelled inside Tara. Without thinking consciously about it, she raised one hand, connecting it sharply with Ryan's cheek.

"How dare you speak to me like that—" she began, but she was given no chance to finish.

Ryan pulled her savagely into his arms, his mouth claiming hers with furious passion.

English author **KRISTY McCALLUM** is happily married to a hero-type husband who teases her because she hasn't yet used him as a model in her books. They have three children and live in Devon. Kristy has a weakness for buying houses that are too big for them, especially neglected-looking houses she can enjoy restoring. So far, her practical husband has kept her from buying a stately home! She is happiest when writing, planning the book in her mind, making her characters come alive and tussling with their tendency to have minds of their own.

KRISTY McCALLUM

Tiger Moon

Harlequin Books

TORONTO • NEW YORK • LONDON
AMSTERDAM • PARIS • SYDNEY • HAMBURG
STOCKHOLM • ATHENS • TOKYO • MILAN
MADRID • WARSAW • BUDAPEST • AUCKLAND

Harlequin Presents first edition October 1992
ISBN 0-373-11500-8

Original hardcover edition published in 1991
by Mills & Boon Limited

TIGER MOON

CHAPTER ONE

'You must be mad! Someone is offering to buy, way over the odds, your shares in your father's company and you're refusing to sell them?'

Tara sighed. 'Why won't you understand? How can I sell those shares without even checking if Daddy approves of the deal?'

'You're still Daddy's girl, aren't you? I would have thought since you've just finished university you would have grown out of that childish hang-up you used to have. Since the divorce he hasn't tried to get in touch with you, yet you still persist in clinging to this naïve belief that he cares for you. . .' Her mother broke off to laugh a little harshly. 'You wouldn't even have any shares in Hall Bay if I hadn't insisted that he made some provision for your future! God knows he tied them up tightly enough, retaining the voting rights on them until you were twenty-one, when they should have been released when you were eighteen!'

Her mother got up and began to walk quickly round the room, her whole attitude one of frustration, obvious to the watching girl. 'Why, Tara? Why this loyalty to a man who has made it abundantly clear that he doesn't care about you any more?'

Tara shrugged her shoulders and looked down at the thick pile of the carpet. She knew it was going to be hopeless to try and put her real thoughts and feelings into words, and she accepted also that if she told her mother the truth, then it was going to cause a row, and rows were things she tried to avoid. . . Oh, well, it seemed she was doomed to go on fighting in this bitter triangle that was the legacy of her parents' divorce.

She took a deep breath. 'Daddy made me promise never to take any drastic decision in my life without first consulting him. He said it didn't matter if we didn't see each other until I was grown up; I was never to forget that I was his daughter, and that he would think about me every single day of his life, and that I was to do the same. . . That way we wouldn't forget each other. He also told me that it would be extremely unlikely that you would ever let me go to Hong Kong to see him, so I was to wait until the time was right. He said I'd know when that was, and when I'd made up my mind he'd pay for my ticket back to Hong Kong.' Tara looked up and risked her mother's expression, then quickly looked away as the normally beautiful features were twisted into a mask of hatred.

'I might have guessed he'd do something like this!' Tara winced at the molten anger that threatened to explode around her head. 'Devious, unscrupulous man, why should I ever have thought he'd let you go?' Her mother suddenly

turned on her. 'You're old enough now to understand why I left him, and made sure I took you
with me! He was keeping a half-Chinese mistress
at the time, and as soon as we were divorced he
intended to marry her!'

Tara shut her eyes. 'Yes, I know, he told me.
You don't have to tell me any more. . .'

It seemed as if her mother didn't hear her. 'I
made him pay for that divorce! The price of his
freedom was parting with shares in his beloved
company, and now you have the chance of making
him pay in full!' Her mother came to stand next to
her, her face now alive with cruel triumph. 'Do
you remember how hard it was when we first got
back to London, darling? I had to go out to work,
and we lived in that poky little flat? I swore then
that one day I'd make him suffer for what he did
to us. . .'

'Come on, Mummy, it wasn't that bad. You're
dramatising it all far too much. Anyway, it wasn't
long before you married John.' The mention of her
stepfather's name did a lot to cool the situation
down.

'John, yes. . . At least he's a great deal richer
and more important than your father will ever be!'

Tara half smiled at her mother's words. John
Chacewater was president of one of the largest
banks in the world, as well as having inherited a
great deal of money of his own. 'Why don't you
forget Daddy, then? Surely he can't matter to you

now—after all, it's been twelve years since the divorce.'

Her mother gave her a look that had her frowning. 'I will never forgive your father for two reasons. First because he always cared far more for his company and his mistresses than he did for me, and secondly because he tried to keep you with him, to be brought up by his whore!' She moved away to stand, casually elegant, by the tall windows of the big London house before turning again to face her daughter. 'If you go back to Hong Kong, don't think you can come back to live here with me! I can guess from your mulish expression that nothing I've said has made the slighest difference, has it?'

Sadly Tara nodded her head.

'If you walk out on me because of some absurd promise you made your father when you were still a child, well, you go for good! People change a great deal, you know, in twelve years. Your father may not be as pleased to see you as you seem to think, so I should be careful if I were you. Not many girls in this world enjoy the sort of lifestyle you've had since I married John.'

'Blackmail?' Tara questioned wrily.

'Just common sense, my dear. I wouldn't depend on that offer for the Hall Bay shares to hold up either. My guess is a take-over is on the cards so you'll be doubly a fool if you don't cash them in.'

'But we don't know who's making the offer!' Tara protested. 'It could be anyone.'

'So, who cares?' her mother replied. 'The word is that they're having a cash-flow problem right now.'

'Where did you hear that?'

'Right here in this house! Oh, not from John, so you needn't think you can get the truth from him. You should know better than most that a great deal of inside information is discussed at my dinner parties! Hall Bay have done very well since your father joined forces with his partner—I gather that since diversifying abroad they've landed themselves with a short-term crisis because they're overstretched. I gather it isn't anything too serious, so maybe it's his partner who's trying to get control. . .' She broke off to smile at the thought before returning to the attack. 'So what's it to be, Tara? Are you going or staying?'

'I have to go, Mummy. I wish you could understand that, because I don't want to seem disloyal.'

'You always were a stubborn little girl! I wish you luck, because I think you're going to need it. Don't be too surprised if your father doesn't welcome you with open arms!'

Tara got off the plane at Kai Tak Airport and was almost overwhelmed by the memories that flooded through her. Hong Kong was flying no flags for her return—the sky was overcast and the humidity high—but the evocative smells and the dramatic skyline had her pulses racing. At last she was home after twelve years of exile!

Impatient at the wait for her luggage, she shook back her shoulder-length tawny hair and moved briskly into the ladies' cloakroom to tidy herself up. Golden eyes shadowed by thick lashes, slightly vulnerable, stared back at her from the mirror. She wrinkled her nose at the sprinkling of freckles that still covered it despite the fact that it had been winter when she left London, and started to carefully make up her face.

Her thoughts were busy as she worked hard at trying to erase the effect of the long flight. She had the high cheekbones beloved of photographers, and a wide mouth too generous for real beauty. She herself considered her looks rather odd, but most people found her face arresting if not downright fascinating. Tall, with slightly opulent curves, she was a deep-bosomed girl who carried herself easily. At sixteen she had been ashamed of her figure but now that she was twenty-one she had come to terms with the fact that most men found it distinctly alluring. Slim-hipped and long-legged, she was used to attracting attention, and her confidence was in itself attractive. Few people guessed that underneath her poise the seeds of insecurity lurked, a dark reminder of her parents' bitter divorce and the role she had been forced to play in it.

Her luggage expertly taken care of by the porter, she scanned the waiting crowd expectantly, but there was no sign of her father. Although he might have difficulty in recognising her, she knew she would know him, and it was with disappointment that she accepted that even now he did not have time to come to the airport himself. She guessed he would send his driver, Mr Chu, so it seemed sensible to wait just inside the glass exit doors in air-conditioned comfort, while she checked the line of cars waiting to pick up the passengers. She tried not to mind the non-appearance of her father, but jet lag combined with fatigue made her view the seething masses of people who jostled and shoved their way around her with jaded eyes. Resentfully she pushed her way forward until she had a clear view of the cars waiting to pick up passengers, her porter following uncomplainingly in her wake. There was no sign of Mr Chu, but she refused to believe that her father would leave her unmet at the airport even if he was unable to come himself.

Her attention was attracted by a man leaning casually against the wall quite near her. He seemed oblivious of the noise and bustle around him, his whole attitude one of intense concentration as he studied her figure, then, belatedly, her face.

Tara fought unsuccessfully to ignore him, then with a mental shrug allowed him to catch her eye. Somewhere in his middle thirties, she guessed, not conventionally good-looking but with such an air of intense vitality that he caught and held attention. The eyebrows were thick over vivid blue eyes, and the nose a little crooked. His hair was a dark auburn, but fine, and fell a little untidily over his forehead. The mouth with the full lower lip was tilted upwards with sudden amusement as he realised he had caught her attention.

Quite suddenly he gave her a smile of great charm, showing white, even teeth. Quite forgetting where she was, she smiled back, all her worries about not being met forgotten. Half of her was instantly appalled; she couldn't imagine why she had allowed herself to respond to his blatant overtones, so she immediately turned away, hoping he hadn't noticed the wave of colour that had swept her face. For all that his was an interesting face although she would have been pushed to explain quite why. She had noticed that his clothes were expensive, yet the grey silk of the suit was slightly crumpled as if he didn't particularly care how he looked. He wasn't a very tall man, about her own height, she guessed, yet there was something in his stance, for all its casualness, that spelled authority, as if he recognised and accepted that he was important. Unable to resist, yet feeling slightly shocked with herself, once more she allowed her eyes to meet his.

He held her rather owlish gaze longer than she found comfortable, so belatedly she raised her eyebrows in faint hauteur to discourage him, before deliberately turning away yet again.

'Miss Halliday?' The voice was warm and deep

with more than a hint of a Welsh lilt. She turned to acknowledge him, but this time her eyes were guarded, showing she felt more than a little wary of him. It had been a shock to hear her name on his lips.

'Yes?'

'My name is Veryan Bay. Your father asked me to come and meet you. Unfortunately he has had to leave for Los Angeles on business.'

Disappointment and curiosity warred within her, momentarily depriving her of speech. Intrigued she began to study him hin return, her extreme tiredness combined with the strong physical awareness between them making him appear in sharp focus as the background blurred around him.

Veryan Bay gave her a quick practised smile. 'I know you must be disappointed, but he shouldn't be away too long.' He seemed to understand that she was at a loss for words because he turned to the patiently waiting porter, indicating that he should follow them outside. 'Chu is here with the car, Miss Halliday—he's looking forward to seeing you again.'

She allowed herself to be shepherded out into the warm humidity towards the large, old-fashioned Rolls-Royce that had belonged to her father as far back as she could remember. She greeted the smart little Chinese man, in his chauffeur's uniform, with pleasure as he bowed deeply in greeting, then grasped his hands tightly, almost overcome with the familiarity of her memories.

'Mr Chu! It's very good to see you again!'

'Yes, missy!' He gave her a large, gap-toothed smile. 'It's been a long time, you just little girl——'

'She's certainly grown a bit since those days!' Veryan interrupted. 'Now let's get moving; I expect Miss Halliday's tired.'

In the back of the car, Tara pulled herself together.

'Veryan. . . That's an unusual name,' she murmured politely, trying to come to terms with the fact that her father was not at home and that her problems would have to be postponed.

'I suppose it is. My parents have always told me that it was because I was conceived on a holiday in Cornwall very near a place of the same name. . .' He grinned at her. 'I suppose they thought it amusing to commemorate such an auspicious event by calling me Veryan, or perhaps to recall happy memories!'

Tara fought hard to keep her colour steady. This man was outrageous, but she couldn't quite stop her mouth from tilting in amusement at his explanation. She made a severe effort with herself and managed to ask, reasonably calmly, 'You are my father's partner?'

One eyebrow rose in surprise at her question. 'Yes,' he drawled slowly, 'although I didn't expect you to know that.'

Tara was suspicious. 'Why ever not?' she queried.

'Your father and I didn't join forces until after you had left Hong Kong, so I can't see any reason why you should know of my existence, any more than I was really aware of you, except as a shadowy figure from the past. By the way, do call me Ryan, and I'll call you Tamara if I may?'

She nodded, then turned away from him, afraid that he might see the pain his unthinking words had brought to her face. Did her father think of her in the same way? Maybe that was why he had left Hong Kong so suddenly. . . She sat up a little straighter and gritted her teeth, memories of some of her mother's last words to her uncomfortably in the forefront of her mind. Nothing was turning out as she had hoped, but this stranger sitting next to her had the uncomfortable power of making her far too aware of him. If he was her father's partner then he must be close to him; it would be better not to show her feelings so clearly in the future, so she made a point of being interested in her surroundings now that they had left the Cross Harbour Tunnel. She could see already that Hong Kong had changed enormously since she had left. There were many more skyscrapers, and, it seemed to her, more people as well as more traffic.

'It changes all the time, you know,' her companion drawled into her ear, and Tara found it impossible to stop her eyes being drawn inexorably to his. 'Although there's only a few more

years to go before the colony is handed back to the
Chinese, we're still building all the time.'

'So I can see,' she replied, a little breathlessly. 'It
shows a great deal of faith in the future, doesn't
it?'

'Not necessarily—it's still possible to borrow
from the banks and get a return before the final
handing over.'

She heard the cynicism in his voice and disliked
it. 'So you're one who doesn't believe there will be
a future under the Chinese?'

'Whatever gave you that idea?'

She now discovered that the laughing blue eyes
could be uncomfortably penetrating, and for the
first time began to realise that this man could be
formidable. 'You sounded so cynical!'

'I didn't mean to, you just jumped to a conclusion. The wrong one.'

'So, Hall Bay are going to stay here?' This time
she didn't have the courage to meet his eyes, so
concentrated on studying his hands, which lay
lightly on his lap. They were a beautiful shape,
with thin, sensitive fingers.

'Indeed they are, for better or for worse as you
might say. Although I think it's prudent to diversify a bit into other countries. We don't want to be
caught with all our eggs in one basket!' The light-
ness was back in his voice and face as he continued. 'Are you interested in the company,
Tamara?'

She shrugged her shoulders, pretending indifference, suddenly wary of his motives, and changed the subject.

'Not really. By the way, are you taking me home?'

'I'm afraid not. Unfortunately your stepmother is also away, visiting her relations, so I wondered if you'd like to stay in one of the company's flats? It's rather small, but I have an apartment in the same block and the couple who work for me will also take care of you, unless, of course, you'd rather stay in a hotel until your father returns?'

Tara lowered her eyes so he wouldn't see the sudden flare of anger that swept through her like a flame. Who was this stranger to stop her staying in her father's house? She'd been looking forward so much to seeing again the home of her childhood, so her voice was cold as she answered. 'It doesn't seem that I've been left with much choice.' She swung her face away from him, afraid that he might see the glitter of tears that made everything swim in front of her eyes.

'Listen, Tamara!' He swung her round to face him. 'Why have you come out here now? For years you've ignored your father, then suddenly, out of the blue, you send him a fax saying you're on your way. . .' He stopped suddenly, and let her go.

Warning lights suddenly flashed large in her mind—she must be careful to give nothing away. 'I owe you no explanations!' She hoped the scorn in her voice would disguise the fact that her brain was working overtime as once again she turned away from him. Was this the man who was behind her sudden trip to Hong Kong? If so she'd better be extremely careful in what she told him.

'No. . .' But his eyes were now as hard and sharp as sapphires. 'You must forgive my curiosity, but if you're honest admit I have reason to be curious.'

Tara hunched her shoulders defensively. 'I admit nothing! Anyway, why should I tell you anything? You're a stranger, and whatever reasons I might have for coming to Hong Kong are nothing to do with you!' She crossed her fingers, and gave a silent prayer that she was right, because if she was wrong, then her father's whole life could be destroyed.

'I wonder,' he replied. 'Don't forget I own half of Hall Bay.'

Tara half froze with shock as she heard the question in his voice. Did that mean he knew about the pressure on her to sell her holding in Hall Bay? What was she to do? Anger longed to make her give him a stinging set-down because he'd obviously been setting her up right from the start when he'd caught her eye so blatantly at the airport. If only her father were here to help her. She bit her lip—she must play it cool until he returned, because he was the only one who could tell her what to do.

She shrugged carelessly, as if his words had no particular interest for her, still keeping her glance away from him. She had a strong feeling that he, too, had reservations about her, and she began to resent his presence next to her.

By now the car had started to ascend the peak, climbing higher and higher, away from the hurrying, busy people who worked in the centre of the town towards comparative peace. The huge skyscrapers were now beneath them, and past and present began to blur in Tara's mind. Everything she had dreamed about for years was now going to be spoilt by his being with her. She felt immensely tired. All her excitement had died away, and she couldn't help wondering if she had just made the biggest mistake of her life as the car purred smoothly into the driveway of a small block of flats. She felt like weeping at the sight; so familiar, yet so different.

She let her head fall back against the soft leather of the seat and shut her eyes. It was too much effort to think and she was too tired.

'You must be exhausted!' Ryan's voice was soft. 'Never mind, it won't be too long now before you can relax. Ah Chee and Ah Woon will have got everything ready for you.'

She allowed him to usher her into the big reception hall and then into the lift, grateful for the support of his arm under hers as she felt rather wobbly and peculiar.

The apartment he showed her into looked charming. There was a beautiful arrangement of flowers on the low table in between two large sofas which had her exclaiming in pleasure.

'It's fairly simple, I'm afraid——' Ryan gestured with his hand '—just this one big room and a couple of bedrooms with bathrooms and a kitchen. Do you think you'll be all right here?'

'I'll be fine. . .' She swayed a little with tiredness.

'You really are done in, aren't you?' Ryan's voice sounded harsh as she turned bewildered eyes to him. 'Ah Woon has left you food, but I suggest you go straight to bed. She'll come down later and unpack for you, and if you can make yourself wake up in time I'll take you out to dinner.'

Grateful for any reprieve, she followed him into the larger of the two bedrooms and collapsed on to the end of the large double bed, which had been turned down in readiness for her arrival, while he dumped her overnight bag on to a chair.

'Sweet dreams!' He gave her a warm smile that had her automatically responding, then he quietly left the room, closing the door behind him. Without wasting any time, Tara removed her clothes and crept between the sheets and was soon dead to the world.

She woke up several hours later alert and much refreshed. She knew exactly where she was, and lay still in the bed thinking back on all the implications and disappointments of her arrival. She guessed it was early evening, and wondered when Ryan had planned to come and collect her. Lazily

she made herself get up and walk through to the
adjoining bathroom to run herself a bath. There
was a great deal to think about but she was
disquieted by the fact that it was Ryan who had
held her thoughts from the moment of waking.

How had she let herself become so obsessed
with a stranger? Bewildered, she went back quietly
in her mind through their conversation a few
hours ago. Why, he had as good as told her that
he was only interested in her because of her shares
in Hall Bay. Yet in spite of that knowledge, which
should make her detest him, here she was, waiting
for him to come and collect her with an eagerness
which she couldn't even disguise from herself.

She left the bedroom quietly, dressed in a soft
yellow cotton dress, her white kid shoes making
little sound as she began to explore her surroundings. The air-conditioning hummed away quietly
as she moved over to the long sliding windows
that gave on to a balcony that appeared to run the
length of the apartment. She resisted the temptation to go outside for the moment as she moved
from room to room. The walls were painted in cool
pastel colours, and the floors were marble with the
occasional beautiful rugs which added rich pools
of colour to the rooms. The two large sofas were
covered in a pale chintz depicting the tree of life,
and the rectangular glass table in front of them
was supported by four pottery elephants in shades
of blue and white.

The air was heavy with the smell of lilies from

the huge bowl of flowers, their scent seductive and Eastern. Her cases were neatly stacked against one wall, but Tara felt disinclined to disturb them at the moment; there would be time for that tomorrow. Restlessly she explored the kitchen, pouring herself a refreshing glass of fresh lime juice from a jug in the fridge. Everything was spotlessly clean, perhaps a little sterile. There were none of the small touches about the place that made somewhere home.

The sliding windows opened noiselessly, allowing her to slip outside where the sudden heat hit her in a moist, warm embrace. She took a deep breath, savouring, remembering. . .then used all her resolution to come to a decision.

'Good evening, Tamara. I hope you feel better after your sleep?'

She swung round quickly, a tall golden girl, her hair a bell of light on her shoulders.

'Mmm, you do look better. . . I expect you're very hungry now, aren't you?' Ryan didn't wait for an answer, just dropped a hand lightly on to her shoulder, ignoring the shudder that went through her at his touch. 'I thought you'd like to eat European food tonight—we don't want to give you too much of a culture shock, do we? I hope so, because I've already booked a table for us at Pierrots. It's supposed to be one of the best restaurants in Hong Kong. As it's at the top of the Mandarin; you should get a good view of all the changes that have taken place since you were last here.'

She was almost perfectly convinced that he didn't expect her to remember anything much about her previous life, but as she didn't intend to accept his invitation she was prepared to let it ride for the moment. His eyes were almost on a level with hers. Part of her mind thought irrelevantly that she would be taller than him if she wore high-heeled shoes. He perhaps had the fractional advantage, but there could be very little in it. She recovered her poise, her senses now doubly alert at his close proximity.

'I would prefer not to eat out tonight, thank you very much.'

He raised his eyebrows, but there was sudden lurking amusement in his eyes. 'I've just been talking to your father. He is delighted you have arrived safely and thinks it's a good idea that we get to know each other until he returns. I don't think he would be very pleased if you were left alone on your first night back in Hong Kong, do you?'

They stood opposite each other, Tara careful to keep the half-wary attraction she felt for him hidden. She was not at all sure that she liked him very much, and she certainly didn't trust him. Yet he stirred her senses in some indefinable way that no man had ever done before. She guessed that he hadn't long stepped out of a shower, because his hair was slicked back tidily, still looking damp.

The jacket of his dark suit hung back to show her the tiny initials VB on his cream silk shirt, and she could smell the fresh tang of aftershave.

Half ashamed of herself and her thoughts, she turned away with sudden determination. Ryan might be attracted to her physically, but that was all. She guessed that in his eyes she was already tarred with the same brush as her mother. 'It's very kind of you to think about entertaining me, Ryan, but it's quite unnecessary, you know. I have some friends out here so you needn't worry about me. In fact I shall enjoy finding my way around again on my own.'

He gave a curiously resigned shrug, then smiled at her. 'It would still give me a great deal of pleasure if you would come out to dinner tonight. Your father is depending on me to look after you, and I wouldn't like to let him down.' She gave him a sharp look which he met with candour. 'We're very old friends, you know, and it would worry him if he thought I had left you here alone.'

Tara debated with herself quickly, then mentally shrugged off her instinctive feeling of danger at spending too much time in this man's company. There were a great many things she needed to find out, and hopefully Ryan would supply some of the answers. 'It's very kind of you. . . All right, then,' she gave him a practised smile, 'thank you very much!'

She knew that he, too, was curious about her,

but she felt strong enough now to parry any too probing questions on his part. The lift in her spirits she put down to happiness at being back where she felt she belonged, and if a traitorous thought warned her that it was because she was going to enjoy crossing swords with Ryan then she firmly squashed it.

'Let's go, shall we?' It seemed he, too, was feeling good, because there was a lazy smile of appreciation as he studied her face and figure slowly and with pleasure.

'When is my father expected to return?'

'In about ten days, we hope, although it could take longer.'

'So long? That's—er—unusual, isn't it? I mean I never remember him leaving the office for more than two or three days. . .'

'Ah, but that was before I joined him!'

'I see.' She bit her lip as she preceded him to the front door. Tara wasn't convinced by the glib answer, and guessed that the rumours she had heard about Hall Bay were perhaps true after all. Certainly her mother had seemed delighted when she had first passed them on to her daughter.

'Hadn't you better collect a wrap or something?' Ryan's voice bought her smartly back to earth. 'The air-conditioning can give you the most frightful cold until your body has adjusted to these constant changes of temperature.'

Furious with herself for forgetting not only a wrap but her bag, she left him while she ran quickly back to her room. She'd been following him meekly, like a lamb to the slaughter, so mesmerised by him and her thoughts that she'd forgotten everything else.

CHAPTER TWO

I⊤ WAS difficult for Tara to hide her tension as Ryan, with smooth, practised charm, took charge of the evening. As they walked across the restaurant towards their table she was aware of the women's eyes following them. Ryan acknowledged one or two greetings, but showed no disposition to introduce her to anyone. She couldn't help overhearing the comments from a couple of men as they passed their table.

'That jet-fresh Doris is quite something, wouldn't you say?'

'Ryan always has all the luck! I wonder how long she's been around?'

Puzzled, Tara attacked her host as soon as they had sat down. 'What does "jet-fresh Doris" mean?'

She saw him grin. 'It's a local expression for any new girls who fly into Hong Kong!' he told her, his eyes full of amusement. 'I wondered if you heard that comment.'

'And how long do they have to be here before they cease to be "jet-fresh"?' she enquired drily.

'A month!'

'I see——' But Ryan wasn't prepared to let her finish. 'If she's quite something, like you, for instance, then you'll soon meet them. It's a pretty small world out here, and fairly cliquey. You'll find that the English stay pretty much together, as do the Americans and the Aussies. I'm not saying the groups never overlap, but you'll find that you mix mostly with the English.'

'Thank you!' she said drily.

'Any time I can be of help——'

It was her turn to interrupt. 'You won't need to bother about me, Ryan. I already have a number of friends out here who I'm looking forward to seeing again.' She got the impression that he wasn't particularly pleased about that, which made her feel a little less at a disadvantage with him, but it didn't last long.

It seemed to her that he went out of his way to amuse and relax her. Although she remained quite aware that he was doing it deliberately, she found it took a considerable amount of effort on her part not to respond too blatantly to the practised approach.

By the end of the meal she was forced to accept that he had an outstandingly charismatic personality, and was quite accustomed to using it to gain his own ends. She was also more aware of him physically than any other man she had met, although she did her best to deny this to herself.

It wasn't until over coffee that he asked her the first personal question. 'I don't suppose you've had to take a job, Tamara?' His eyes slid over her body and face again quite openly. 'Anyway, you look far too beautiful to be associated with anything as boring as work!'

Underneath the teasing note in his voice she detected the determination to find out about her. 'A lily of the field?' she queried wrily, then shook her head. 'No, I don't think I'd qualify for that remarkably boring job! Actually I've just finished taking a degree in business studies at university.'

She watched with amusement as he choked into his coffee. 'Good God,' he spluttered, 'but you're only just twenty-one!'

'It's quite possible to get a degree in three years,' she told him kindly. 'I started immediately I left school.' She rather enjoyed the slightly shattered expression on his face until it changed to wary respect. The relaxed and casual atmosphere he had created so successfully between them at dinner was now over. Tamara mentally girded her loins for the inquisition she knew was to come.

'Just why have you come to Hong Kong now, Tamara?'

The blunt question made her play a little for time. 'Do call me Tara! Everyone else does. . .' She picked up her coffee-cup and slowly sipped the hot strong liquid before answering. 'I've come back to Hong Kong because that's where I feel I belong,' she told him slowly, her eyes holding his disbelieving ones.

'That's strange,' he countered, 'I would have thought you would have forgotten most of your life here.'

'Would you?' She gave him a non-committal smile. 'Well, you're wrong, because I remember it all very well indeed!' She sat back in her chair, watching his expression with sudden irritation. 'What exactly do you want to know about me?' she demanded sarcastically.

She had the satisfaction of seeing that she had slightly disconcerted him. 'I'm sorry, I don't mean to sound rude, but naturally I'm curious. Your father I count as one of my greatest friends, so of course we all want to know what happened to you after you left Hong Kong.'

She didn't like the cynical smile on his face, but chose to ignore it. 'Not a great deal,' she answered drily. 'I was sent away to boarding-school pretty quickly, and after my mother married John Chacewater I lived with them in London. He has an apartment in New York as well, but I wasn't often over there with them.'

'Do you get on with your stepfather?'

'Yes, I suppose so—I didn't see a great deal of him, but he was always kind. He works extremely hard, you see, so there never was a lot of time left over for family.'

He gave her a practised smile, but she felt again the sharpness of his attention. 'Is that why you took a degree in business studies, because your stepfather recommended it?'

'Partly, yes. He approves of women having careers, always supposing they want one, that is.'

'Then he's unusual for a man of his generation!'

'Possibly.' She smiled. 'Anyway, he offered me a job if I got my degree.'

'And will you work for him?'

'Ah! Well, I'm not quite sure at the moment if the offer will still be open.'

'Why ever not?'

She gave him a scornful look. 'Because my mother's not too pleased at my rather sudden decision to come out here and see my father!' And that's the understatement of the year, she added silently, remembering the final scene between them.

'Do you get on with your mother?'

Tara began to resent his blunt, probing questions. 'We have different interests,' she parried lightly, 'and now can we talk about you for a change? Why did you join forces with my father?'

He didn't appear to mind the change of subject. 'It seemed the sensible thing to do as we worked in certain areas that overlapped.' He gave her another of his lazy smiles. 'We were already friends,' he finished smoothly.

'There's quite an age-gap between the two of you, surely?'

'We've never found it a problem,' he answered gravely, but she was all too aware of his amusement. 'In fact it's been a great success on the whole. Our shared interests have amalgamated very well.'

Tara thought she could detect a faintly patronising air about him and disliked it. 'That was lucky for you, wasn't it? It must have been a great help to tap into the resources of an already well-established company. . .' She made no attempt to hide her casual contempt, deliberately trying to provoke him into an indiscretion.

'So that's what you think happened!' The voice was soft, but the eyes were ice-cold. 'I can assure you our companies merged on equal terms.' She was reminded uncomfortably of an animal about to spring on its prey. The leashed force of his personality, held in check only by a formidable will, suddenly frightened her. This man was more than capable of starting a successful company in the cut-throat jungle of international business. She guessed that she had seriously underrated him.

He mustn't know how disconcerted she felt, so she sat up straighter, then raised her eyebrows in surprise. 'Lucky Daddy! It's unusual to find two equally successful companies prepared to join forces.' She was quietly pleased that her voice showed no sign of strain, but it was going to be hard to keep up this appearance of cool disinterest. Phrases like letting sleeping tigers lie swam unbidden into her mind, so she stood up gracefully, and smiled, 'Please excuse me for a minute.'

'Of course!' He too rose to his feet and moved the chair back for her, but she didn't altogether trust his smile as she left the room.

Alone in the cloakroom she let her breath out in a sigh of relief. Had she just gone too far? She shook her head in denial. No, it had certainly provoked Ryan into showing his true colours. She had come back to Hong Kong to see her father again, sure of her welcome because it was in her power to save his company. She had booked her flight out in heady exhilaration without thinking of anything else, supremely happy because chance had given her the perfect excuse to be with him again.

Tamara's adamant refusal to even consider selling her shares had irritated her mother to the point of recklessness on her last night at home. John Chacewater, unable to stop either of them, had shrugged his shoulders and left the room. It had been as if his going released the last of her mother's inhibitions.

'I don't understand how you can be so stupid and disloyal!' her mother shouted at her. 'You can get a fortune for those shares, and what's more it will make your father finish with that damned company that he cared far more about than you or I!'

'For heaven's sake, Mummy, why be so vindictive?'

Tara was shocked to see her mother's face change again from its normal, serene beauty into a ugly mask of hate. 'You know perfectly well why I feel as I do. Anyway, he was never around when I needed him—never! And when he was at home he spent most of his time with you!'

Tara recoiled slightly from the malevolent jealousy that now seemed to be directed towards her.

'Oh, come on! You were never around, always out somewhere.' She felt the need to be defiant somehow, to fight the ugly emotions that threatened to overcome her.

'Yes, I was, and who could blame me for that? Oh, I was so bored in Hong Kong. A horrid, provincial little town for all its surface glamour. I begged your father to return to London—anywhere! But no, my thoughts and wishes weren't important—I don't think they ever were to him!'

'Well, I got my own back in the end. He could stay if he wanted to, but if he wanted to get rid of me then he could pay the price! He lost total control of his beloved company, and he lost his daughter!'

Tara was suddenly sure that her mother didn't realise who she was talking to. 'Did he want to keep his child?' she queried, softly.

'Yes, he wanted her, but she was my daughter as well! Why should I leave her behind to be brought up by some Chinese woman? I made sure once we were back in London that he'd have no more contact with her!'

Tara felt like being sick at the gloating expression of satisfaction on her mother's face. 'You never once thought about me!' she screamed. 'I never wanted to be with you! You never had any time for me, but he did. He cared for me, I know he did, but you didn't, did you?' She didn't wait for an answer. 'You were always too busy with your parties and your clothes, and you thought of me as a nuisance! You knew how unhappy I was back here but you didn't care! All you thought about was getting your own back. You've kept me from him all these years, and I never knew. . .' She buried her face in her hands, almost overcome with misery.

'Tamara! How dare you speak to me like that? You've had everything you could possibly want——'

'Except my father!' she interrupted.

'What's he ever done for you?' her mother snapped back.

'Loved me, perhaps,' Tara answered quietly, and her eyes were hard and unforgiving as she searched her mother's face, but the serene and beautiful mask was back in place.

'So you think I don't care for you at all. How juvenile, Tamara!'

But she wasn't quite back under control, her daughter noticed, because two spots of natural colour showed through the careful make-up.

'Not really. . .' Tara's voice was cool as she continued, 'I think you're too selfish to care for anyone very much, except perhaps John, and only because he gives you what you want.'

For a moment she thought her mother was going to hit her, then the clenched hands loosened to fall by her sides. Her face was now a cold mask of dislike. 'I see I should have left you behind after all! What a pity I didn't because after all we don't have much in common, do we?'

The ugly truth should have frightened her, but somehow it didn't. She felt a great sense of sadness, almost despair, that she could never have been the child her mother wanted. Although it was painful, there was also a sense of release, so, quite incapable of words, she just nodded.

'I suppose I can't change your mind?'

'I must see him again,' Tara told her mother quietly. They were both quiet for a moment, deep in their own thoughts, but it was Patricia Chacewater who broke the silence between them.

'Brave words, Tamara! But if you go it means you won't be able to come back here. I meant that, you know, when we first discussed this whole problem. If you go back to Hong Kong then as far as I'm concerned you're finished. I hope you understand?' She accepted the quiet nod with a thinning of her mouth. 'I wonder if you really do?' she mused, before continuing, 'Perhaps it will after all be a good thing for you to find out how most people have to live their lives. . .' She stood up gracefully and moved towards the door. 'Your life has been a very easy one so far, Tamara—I hope you won't live to regret this decision of yours!' On this valedictory note she'd given her daughter a last smile, then with a curious gesture of her hands, as if she were washing her only child out of her life, she had left the room.

Tara was brought to her senses by a party of giggling Chinese women who crowded into the ladies'. She had no idea how long she'd been in

there, but it seemed a good idea to get back to
Ryan. He was no longer sitting at their table, but
the manager told her he'd had to make a call, and
would she wait for him in the bar next to the
restaurant?

Grateful for this reprieve, she was conducted to
a small table that overlooked the centre of the town
with distant views of the port. The huge skyscrapers glowed with lights, like overgrown
Christmas trees, and at street level flashing neon
signs, glittering in all colours of the rainbow, called
the people to come and sample their hidden
delights. Shopping complexes, restaurants, night-
clubs—the lateness of the hour didn't seem to
matter. If you wanted to buy something, eat, or
dance, then they were ready to sell. The warm
dark velvet of the night didn't really stand a chance
as the town glittered with radiant life.

A small bottle of champagne was brought over
to her table, and without waiting for her per-
mission the Chinese waiter expertly opened it and
poured her a glass before leaving her alone.

'It's Tamara, isn't it? I wonder if you remember
me?'

The soft Australian accent, combined with
genial, round-faced charm, clicked in her memory.
'Why, yes,' she smiled, 'it's Brett Moncrieff, isn't
it?'

'Clever girl! I thought my days of making an
impression on anything as young and beautiful as
you were long over.' He smiled. 'Mind if I join

you? Or will the boyfriend tear me limb from limb when he gets back?'

She laughed happily. 'No boyfriend, just my father's partner. He's keeping an eye on me until Daddy gets back, and, yes, do join me.'

He sat down next to her. 'This is a bit sudden, isn't it? I don't believe you mentioned you were going on a trip when we last met at your stepfather's house.'

'It's a sort of twenty-first birthday present I'm giving myself, and I suppose it has been done on the spur of the moment. . .' She was silent for a moment trying to think of the right words. 'I was born over here, and I've always wanted to come back. It just seemed the right time to do it.'

'Good for you! But you ought to go on now you've made it this far. Come and see us in Perth. We'll give you a good time and show you a bit of the country!'

'Give me a chance! I only arrived this morning.'

He grinned. 'Sorry. But don't forget, will you? Here. . .' he put his hand into his jacket pocket and brought out a card '. . .this has got my private number on it, and whoever answers always knows where I am. Give a call when you're ready to move on and we'll send the plane up to get you!'

Tara looked her surprise. Brett Moncrieff was one of Australia's most successful tycoons with business interests around the world. He was so important that when he had come to dinner her mother had claimed all his attention. She knew he was not the type of man to casually invite just anyone to his home, and couldn't help wondering just what was behind his invitation.

It seemed he could read her mind, because he grinned. 'No strings, I promise!'

'It's very kind of you——' she began, doubtfully, but he interrupted.

'Nonsense, it would be a pleasure. Any chance of your having dinner with me? I'm here on business for the next week or so if you're not too booked up?'

Relieved that this was something she could happily cope with, she smiled her agreement. Brett Moncrieff was not the sort of man who pounced, she was fairly sure, and even if he was having John Chacewater as a stepfather would make him think twice about doing anything to annoy her in that respect. All the same, as she scribbled down the name of the block of flats where she was staying, and her number, she still had a tiny niggling of doubt about why such an important man was bothering with her.

'Great! I'll give you a call when I know I'm free, and we'll arrange a fun evening.' He stood up. 'Now I'd better get back to my companion in case he thinks I'm going to desert him for the rest of the night!'

Disconcerted, she turned in her seat to look back at the bar to meet Ryan's wary blue gaze as he watched her companion walk away from her to join a tall man sitting with a group of Chinese businessmen. He moved over to join her at a leisurely pace, sliding into the chair left vacant by Brett Moncrieff with all the grace of a large cat.

'Sorry I had to leave you.' He gave a smile which didn't quite reach his eyes. 'An old friend?'

'What? Oh, no, not particularly, I've met him a couple of times with my stepfather, that's all.' She felt confused suddenly, almost as if she had been caught out in some wrongdoing, yet that casual encounter with Brett Moncrieff could hardly have been more innocent on her part.

'Are you going to meet him again?'

Tara's confusion changed explosively to righteous anger. 'What possible concern could it be of yours if I do?' She didn't care that her voice trembled under the indignation she was feeling.

He shrugged lightly before replying. 'I suppose I see myself as standing *in loco parentis*——'

'You what?' Tara didn't even wait for him to finish speaking. 'How dare you speak to me like that? I'm over twenty-one, and if I should ever need advice from anyone older you can rest assured that you'd be the last person I'd come to!'

'Why?'

His query took the wind from her sails, and she allowed her eyes to take in the expression of enigmatic blandness that masked his face. Her rage retreated as caution made her careful of her answer. 'You should know perfectly well,' she told him coldly. 'As far as I'm concerned you are a complete stranger. Why should I trust you? I know

nothing about you!' Warned by the sudden light
in his eyes she continued fiercely, 'Just because
my father made you his business partner does
not—I repeat not—give you the right to interfere
in my life in any way!'

He gave her a sudden grin, throwing up his
hands in mock surrender. 'All right, all right! But
you should lose your temper more often. It suits
you!' He stood up. 'Come on, let's get out of here
and I'll take you dancing.' He held his hand out to
her, persuasively. 'My guess is you're really beginning to wake up right now, so let's go over to
Kowloon and have a good time, shall we?'

Tara fought a fierce war with herself as she tried
to resist the sudden warm friendliness that
showed itself behind those too-knowing eyes that
seemed to take far too much pleasure in studying
her figure so blatantly. She stood up slowly, giving
him a quick practised smile. 'No, I don't think so,
thank you very much, not tonight. I would prefer
to go back to the flat.'

He didn't appear to be too cast down as he
smiled at her, and she was left with the uncomfortable impression that he had managed to follow all
her thought processes. 'Another time, I hope?' he
said easily, as his hand slid smoothly under her
elbow to pilot her towards the lifts, but she
couldn't help noticing that he positioned himself
carefully so she would have no clear view of the
bar and Brett Moncrieff's party.

She made no attempt to invite him into the flat

for a nightcap, even though he had courteously opened the door for her. They stood for a moment looking at each other, Tara slightly defiant, Ryan lazily amused. The amusement deepened as she made no move to leave him. 'I quite agree,' he told her softly, 'this is no way to end an evening. . .' But even as he leant forward to pull her close to him, she moved smartly out of his way.

'I'm waiting for the keys, Ryan!' She noticed the fleeting expression of respect that crossed his face before he grinned at her.

'Sorry!' He handed them over.

'This is the only set you have?' she enquired sweetly. The respect on his face deepened.

'The only set. The caretaker has some though in case you lose them.'

'Don't worry, I shall be careful. Thank you very much for a pleasant evening.' She held out her hand, but he disconcerted her by bending to give it a light kiss before turning back towards the lift. It was with relief that Tara finally closed the door on him, leaning back on its smooth mahogany surface to let her breath out in a long sigh.

At last, quite unable to stop him taking over her mind, she allowed herself to think about her father's partner. Ryan Bay, whom she'd dangerously underestimated. She wondered why she had allowed herself to dismiss him as someone of no account—probably because of loyalty, she told herself. She hadn't wanted to admit that Hall Bay owed him anything; she had preferred to think of its success as all her father's work. And it had been a success, in spite of its present problems. The only contact she had ever managed to keep with her father had been by reading about the business in the financial reports in the newspapers.

She wondered now if the company had gained its present eminence because of Ryan's dynamic personality, and began uncomfortably to think that that was all too probable. She was also under no illusions about why he had bothered to take her out to dinner and had gone to such pains to house her in one of the company's flats. Tonight had just been the opening round, both of them wary, circling each other like boxers in a ring at the start of a fight. She sensed his interest in her was because he knew all too well that she owned a quarter-share in Hall Bay. Was he the anonymous bidder?

She was disturbed from her thoughts by the sound of the phone. Reluctantly, her brows drawn together in a frown, she moved to answer it. Who, apart from Ryan, knew where she was?

'Tara?'

'Yes?'

'Hello, darling, this has been a surprise for us all! I'm sorry I wasn't able to welcome you myself.'

'Oh Daddy!' The sound of her father's voice nearly made her burst into tears. 'I suppose I should have given you more warning, but there wasn't time.'

'Don't worry! As long as you don't rush off
again before I get back——'

'There's no chance of that!' she interrupted.
'When are you coming home?'

'I'm not quite sure at the moment, but I'll do my
best to hurry things up! Now tell me, is this an
extended holiday you're having?'

'No, not exactly—I was hoping to find a job out
here, then when that's set up find myself somewhere to live.'

There was a small silence. 'Does that mean that
you've left home?'

Slightly disconcerted by the sharpness of her
father's query, she answered slowly. 'I'd rather
thought of it the other way round—I mean I hoped
I was coming home. . .'

Tara wasn't sure if she actually heard the sigh of
relief but his next words were a confirmation.
'Bless you, darling! I wasn't sure, it's been so long
since we've been in touch. . . Well, things could
have changed. I wouldn't have blamed you, you
know. Twelve years is a very long time. . .' Unspoken words lay between them, and Tara, filled
with emotion and gratitude, knew that even now
her father would not stoop to denigrate her mother
to her in any way.

She sniffed, and put up a hand to wipe away
the tears. 'Oh, Daddy!' But she wasn't capable yet
of speech.

It seemed that he understood, but his own voice
didn't sound any too steady as he continued, 'This

is not how I'd planned to welcome my daughter home! I'm afraid I'm stuck in LA until I can finalise a deal. It's very important, Tara, otherwise I'd be home on the next plane. I want you to understand that.'

The urgency in Seb Halliday's voice helped to pull her together. 'Of course I do! Don't think about it any more. Daddy, I have to tell you why I'm here. There's been an offer for my shares.'

'You haven't already sold them?' There was no mistaking the sound of panic.

'As if I would before I'd talked to you! Do you know who wants them?'

'Thank God! I tried to call you on your birthday, but I was told you weren't available.'

'Oh, lord! That was Mummy, I expect. She's not best pleased I'm here.'

'No, I'm sorry, baby. I suppose I hoped that the years might have softened her attitude, particularly since she has married again so successfully.'

'Not a hope,' Tara replied more cheerfully, 'she's still the same!'

'Does that mean you've burnt your boats behind you coming out to me?'

'More or less. Don't worry, Daddy. I'd have come sooner if I could, but it seemed sensible to wait until I had my degree, then I could be independent.'

'It seems to me that I have a daughter I can be very proud of. . . I shall have to try to live up to her!'

Tara laughed. 'I'm so pleased to be back in Hong Kong. You don't know how much I've missed you!'

'Nothing like as much as I've missed you! I've tried several times to see you when I've been in London, but sadly it's never been possible. Oh, well, I suppose it never does any good to look back, but there have been many times when I've bitterly regretted allowing your mother to have sole custody of you. It seemed the natural thing to do at the time, but I never thought she would keep up the vendetta against me for so long.' She heard him sigh. 'Well, what's past is past, I suppose— now we must look to the future!'

'Daddy, is the company in trouble?'

'Not really, not on the bottom line, but we are having cash-flow problems because of our policy of diversifying our interests. That's why I'm in LA at the moment, arranging an extended bank loan. Unfortunately it seems that someone is trying to profit from our temporary difficulties.'

'Do you know who?' Tara enquired.

'That's proving a little more difficult to find out than I'd hoped. There's been quite a run on our shares, but they're being bought up by nominees. You do realise that if you sold out now you could make yourself quite a wealthy woman?'

'That message has been thoroughly drummed into me these last few days,' Tara answered drily, 'but I'd rather hang on to them and maybe twist your arm for a job?'

Her father laughed with relief. 'Well, that's easily solved. You can come and work for us at Hall Bay. Sam, our PR girl, has just had to leave, and as I gather you've got your degree in business studies—well, it could be a start for you until you really find out what you want to do.'

'That's a great idea! By the way, how did you know my degree was in business studies?'

'Because I've just been talking to Ryan. He told me you were in the flat. And how are you two getting on?'

Her father's question totally disconcerted her. What was she to tell him? That neither of them trusted the other an inch? That she had suspicions he might be trying to get total control of Hall Bay behind her father's back? 'All right. He took me out to dinner.'

Sebastian Halliday must have heard the reservations in her voice, because he sounded a little relieved as he said, 'Do I gather you aren't likely to fall victim to all that fatal charm?'

This was another poser. Then she decided that there was nothing wrong with the truth. 'I shouldn't think so. It wouldn't do much good if I did because he seems to have doubts about what sort of girl I am!'

'Doubts? Nonsense, you've got too much imagination.'

He sounded disconcerted and a little upset, and she wondered why he seemed so keen to brush aside her words. Upset herself, she decided it was impossible to talk like this; they needed to be face to face.

'Daddy, do you really mean it about the job?'

'I can't think of anything nicer!' he responded quickly.

'What about Ryan? Will he mind, do you think?'

Her father laughed. 'I shouldn't think so—it was his idea in the first place.'

'Ryan's idea?'

'Yes! Don't sound so surprised. The job entails working closely with him, anyway, to start with. He tells me you've grown into a beautiful girl, and we both think it's about time Hall Bay started to project a more glamorous image! We've expanded a great deal in the last few years, so this could be quite an interesting job for you to find your feet in the business world. Anyway, more importantly, it will give us both a chance to get to know each other quickly again, don't you agree?'

She was left with the feeling that both she and her father had been outmanoeuvred, but there was little that could be done about it anyway at the moment, so she accepted gracefully.

'Bless you! As a more than interested party, it's about time you really learnt about the company. It's my considered opinion, by the way, that if you hang on to those shares they'll be worth a great deal more in five years' time! Goodnight, darling, try to get some sleep. Don't think about starting work until you've had enough holiday getting to know Hong Kong all over again. I'll open an account for you in the Royal Bank. If you've just forked out for your ticket, I don't suppose you're feeling too rich! Anyway, they'll get in touch with you, and in the meantime treat Ryan as your banker.'

The line went dead, and Tara slowly replaced the receiver, wondering why her father had never considered that it could be his partner who was trying to gain control of the company.

CHAPTER THREE

TARA spent most of the next few days as far away from the apartment as possible. She needed the time to try and sort out her thoughts, away from Ryan and his disastrous charm. Disastrous it was as far as she was concerned, because it seemed to her that her body and mind were at war with each other over him. Part of her had no reservations about him at all; any time she conjured up his physical presence she became sinkingly aware of his attraction for her. She did her best to fight this awareness, which she was fairly sure he shared, because she was still deeply suspicious about his reasons for trying to keep track of her movements. She knew perfectly well that he was beginning to find her elusiveness irritating; anyway, she was running out of excuses.

Logic had also told her that as far as Hall Bay was concerned he couldn't be acting entirely on his own. Ryan Bay might be a wealthy man on paper, but she was fairly sure he wasn't in the league of the really big asset-strippers, so there had to be someone else involved.

She had a surprising number of friends in the colony. Not from her youth so much as people she had met in London and at school. Nearly all her friends tried to travel, and most seemed to use Hong Kong as a good jumping-off ground for seeing the world. Local gossip had managed to give her quite a considerable insight into Ryan's life. She hadn't really needed telling that he had a considerable reputation as a ladies' man, the latest in a long line being Samantha, an Australian girl who had had the job of PR girl at Hall Bay, who had just returned to Sydney, and whose job Tara had agreed to take over.

She had been extremely careful not to voice her suspicions, but most of the people she talked to didn't seem to know the company had any problem other than a minor cash-flow crisis after investing heavily in Singapore. She found that very interesting. Whoever wanted control of Hall Bay was playing his cards very close to his chest.

She was out on her balcony relaxing, waiting for him to find her early one evening, when the doorbell went. She'd already decided that there was no more point in trying to run—Hong Kong was too small.

'Hi!' she gave him her warm smile, trying to make up for her earlier churlishness, as she answered the door. If she was going to spend time with him at work then they would both have to try to put their personal differences to one side. 'Come in and I'll get you a drink.'

'Something long, cool and non-alcoholic would be perfect.' His answering smile was as warm as hers had been as he followed her out on to the

balcony and settled himself in the lounger next to
hers. He had shed his jacket and tie, and she could
see the dark hairs on his chest through the thin
silk of his shirt. His hair flopped untidily over his
face and his whole appearance was one of
crumpled weariness. Tara was appalled and
ashamed at the feeling of pure unadulterated lust
that swept through her at the sight of him.

'I won't be a minute,' she promised, running
lightly into the kitchen to get some fresh juice for
them both. She was wearing a pair of shorts and a
skimpy T-shirt covered in the bright, primary
colours of a Ken Done design that showed off her
long-legged figure to perfection. She had adapted
remarkably quickly to the humid warmth, and she
glowed with health as she returned with the
frosted glass filled with fresh lime juice.

He toasted her with his eyes. 'I see the heat
doesn't seem to worry you unduly.'

'No,' she smiled, 'I enjoy it, although it's better
up here on The Peak than down there.' She
gestured downwards where the huge skyscrapers
stood, like giant teeth, beneath them. Further out,
across Victoria Harbour, the Star Ferry was making
its way slowly across the sea, its wake creaming
whitely behind it.

'I've tried to get in touch with you several times,
but it seems that you're always out.'

Tara laughed. 'I did tell you that I had lots of
friends here, and there's so much I have to catch
up on——'

'You're not lonely up here all by yourself?' he interrupted.

'No, not at all, I've been too busy.'

'We're expecting your father back early next week.'

'Yes, Serena told me.'

'You've been in touch with Serena?' He looked at her with surprise.

'Yes, why not? I was always very fond of her as a child. Anyway, she's my stepmother. She wants me to move back into our old home, but I don't think that would be a good idea, do you?'

She was amused to see him look disconcerted, as if he wasn't quite sure what to answer. 'I suppose it's still your home, and perhaps your father would like it.'

'No, I don't think it would be right. After all, it's her home now, and I don't think she would really enjoy having a stepdaughter living with her permanently, particularly as we've never shared a house.'

He looked thoughtful. 'I've never thought of it that way, and I'm sure she hasn't either. After all, she's half Chinese, and to them family is very important. She might even be offended and upset if you didn't return.'

'Not if I handle it right.' Tara smiled. 'I think she might even be relieved!'

'You're a strange girl, Tara. Are you always so careful of other people's feelings?'

'Given the chance, then yes. I was brought up

under the principle of "do as you would be done by".'

She knew she had aroused his curiosity, but hoped he wouldn't bring up the subject of her father.

'That doesn't sound like anything I've ever heard about your mother. From all I've gathered over the years she was a monument to selfishness, thinking of no one but herself.'

'But I was brought up by Nanny, and my father had far more time for me when I was little than my mother.'

'*Touché*!' He held up a hand. 'I didn't mean to sound so personal, Tara.'

She shrugged her shoulders. 'I don't mind, anyway it's the truth, I suppose. She's a fairly amazing woman in her way, and she's been a wonderful wife to John. She's just not cut out to be a mother.'

'You're very forgiving!'

Again she shrugged. 'Now, yes, because I think I understand her, but it wasn't always that way.'

'No. . .' He looked at her consideringly. 'I think perhaps you've had a raw deal in life so far.'

She was disconcerted by his percipience and touched on the raw by what she had inadvertently let him see. 'Poor little rich girl?' she jeered. 'Is that what you think I am?'

'No, I don't think that at all! I think you're lucky enough to have the character and personality to build on your misfortunes rather than letting them put you at a disadvantage. In that way you're very like your father, because he's always been ready to learn from his own and other people's mistakes.'

Again Tara was disconcerted, but she'd had enough of this conversation and turned it into other channels. 'Daddy seems to think it might be a good idea if I came to work for Hall Bay. What do you think?'

'I think it would be a very good idea too—if you're willing, that is?'

'Yes, I think I would enjoy it very much.'

'I think you'll learn quickly if you want to, but you did tell me on the way home from the airport that you weren't interested in the company.'

She might have guessed that he'd have one of those inconvenient sort of memories that picked up every little mistake. 'Did I?' she answered vaguely. 'Perhaps I was tired at the time. . .' Deliberately she didn't enlarge her answer, hoping he'd let it go, and she let her breath out silently in relief as he changed the subject.

'Are you interested in sailing?' he queried idly before putting down the now empty glass on the table beside him.

'I've never really done any. Can I get you another drink?'

'No, sit still. I like relaxing next to pretty girls after a hard day's work!' He gave her a grin. 'Would you like to come out with me this weekend? We won't do anything too strenuous, but it can be fun to potter around the islands and the weather forecast is quite good.'

'Yes, I'd love to, if I wouldn't be a nuisance.'

'Don't sell yourself short, Tara! Most men would be more than happy to have your company, even if we find you're seasick right from the word go.' His eyes told her better than words that he wanted her to go with him. Perhaps keeping her distance these last few days had made him more interested? Firmly she tried to squash the thought down.

'That's one thing I can promise you I'm not. I might not know a great deal about sailing, but I have been out in a boat before.'

'Great! You can learn as we go along.' He noticed her apprehensive expression and laughed. 'Don't worry—I can handle her myself if I have to, but you'll soon pick up the hang of it. Sailing is my one relaxation.'

After he had gone, she sat quite still, deep in thought. To start with she tried to be honest with herself, and the conclusion she came to was deeply disturbing. She had met Ryan precisely three times but already the thought of his not being around in the foreseeable future upset her. She knew he didn't trust her, yet that didn't seem to matter. She could make a pretence of fighting him, or disliking him, but that was all it would be, a sham. She knew she was probably being as silly as countless other girls in his past, but as far as he was concerned physically she had no defence at all.

It was all quite simple. She wanted him, wanted to feel his body on hers, and the primitive emotions he had aroused in her would quite likely mean nothing to him. No wonder all those friends of hers raved about him. At first sight he was an unlikely candidate for any girl's interest—not particularly tall, not good-looking, untidy—yet he had managed to catch and hold her interest right from their very first meeting. His voice reminded her of someone, and she searched her memory for the elusive link. Of course! It was the late Richard Burton, the actor. Ryan used his voice for effect; it was an extremely potent weapon, and she was quite sure he knew exactly what he was doing when he exercised all his charm on unsuspecting victims.

She was also fairly certain that he was going to use her for his own ends. She had shares in Hall Bay, and he was unlikely at this particular time to let her run free. He had too much to lose if she should decide to sell to the highest bidder. He was going to stick close to her, far too close for her own comfort, and her only, pathetic, defence was that she knew what he intended.

She was waiting for him the next morning in another of her Ken Done beach outfits, and she noticed he blinked slightly at the outrageous colours.

'I see you're taking precautions that I'll find you again if you fall overboard,' he told her, ruefully.

'Don't you like it?' she asked innocently, awaiting his answer with interest.

'Not many girls could get away with it, but I have to admit——' his eyes moved lingeringly over the pale gold tan of her legs '—that you can!'

Tara had chosen the brash outfit deliberately. These were her fighting colours; she wasn't prepared to slide, softly and gently, into the pit he was digging for her. The whole effect screamed, 'Look at me!' and it took a particular kind of courage to wear it, although she knew she looked good in it. Nobody who saw her today with Ryan was likely to forget her, and it gave her confidence. In the coming battle between them she was going to have to fight her own weaknesses rather than his, so she needed all the help she could get, and that meant looking and feeling good.

'You'll get used to it,' she told him kindly, 'although I suppose to someone of your generation I do look a bit way out.' She bit back a smile at having disconcerted him. 'Shall we go?'

Ryan kept his small yacht in the Royal Hong Kong Yacht Club on Kellet Island. Judging by the speed with which he organised himself, Tara guessed that he was keen to waste no time hanging around being social. In no time, it seemed to her, he had cast off, and with the engine chugging they were on their way. Her first job was to stand in the prow with a boathook, making sure they didn't hit any other boats moored in the marina until they were out into Victoria Harbour.

Soon the serious business of raising the sails took place. She got yelled at a few times for not obeying the shouted orders, but then she wasn't always sure exactly what he was talking about. He had given her the tiller and told her to head the boat into the wind, but she was relieved when he came back to take over. It was exhilarating when they were under sail and she felt free to relax with him.

'I thought we'd sail right around Hong Kong Island, that's why I wanted an early start this morning. Have you ever been to Po Toi?'

'I don't think so—I can't remember.'

'Only about two hundred people live on it, but there's a fish restaurant which is quite good. A sampan will come and meet us when we get to the bay to take us ashore. I expect there'll be other yachts doing the same thing. There isn't much to see on it, apart from the curious rock carvings, and there's supposed to be a haunted house, if you believe in that sort of thing.' He gave her a smile.

'Sounds fun.' She smiled in answer, rather enjoying their close proximity as the Impala lifted herself easily over the swell of the sea. The boat was called *Primavera*, and she thought that was a good name because of the eager way the boat leapt to the wind, rather like a young animal. To her, spring was associated with leaping life.

There was only a faint haze and the sun soon began to burn through strongly. Tara decided she needed some more sun-cream, and went down the hatch to find her bag. She was wearing a plain sky-blue one-piece swimsuit underneath her shorts and top, and decided it was time to strip off. She tied her hair up in a silk scarf to protect if from the sun, then went up again to join Ryan.

'That's better!' he told her admiringly, but there was a teasing look in his eyes. 'If you take the tiller for a moment, I'll help put some cream on your back. I wouldn't want you to get burnt!' He had stripped down to just a pair of white shorts and a white hat, but his skin was deeply tanned and obviously used to exposure to the sun. Wordlessly she came to sit next to him as he told her how to keep the small yacht steady, then he began to massage her back, his hands moving slowly, too easily over her skin. She gritted her teeth and tried not to tense up but Ryan seemed to believe in doing a job thoroughly as his fingers followed and explored her spinal column, up to her neck and shoulders.

'Relax,' he told her, 'I'm not going to bite, and you're terribly tense. . .'

'I thought you were just going to rub on some sunscreen, not give me a massage!' she responded, trying to jerk away from him.

'Most people enjoy being massaged,' he teased, but his hands stilled before dropping.

Tara breathed a sigh of relief. 'I'm not "most people",' she answered drily.

'You can say that again! You remind me at the

moment of a particularly luscious apricot—one just waiting to be picked.'

'Not by you,' she managed to answer calmly.

'Why not? Is there someone else?'

She grabbed at this straw like a drowning woman. 'Yes, there is.'

'How can he bear to let you out of his sight?' he mused. 'Now if you were mine. . .' He left the end of the sentence open, but the air was suddenly heavy with innuendo.

Tara tried to bring the subject back to more mundane matters. 'How long till we get to Po Toi?'

'It's three or four hours' sailing time from Hong Kong. In this wind, probably only three. What's his name?'

'Why should I tell you?' she riposted, trying to gain time.

'I can't think of any reason why not, unless you're ashamed of him.' He had covered his eyes with dark glasses, but she knew he was trying to provoke her into an indiscreet answer.

'I'm not ashamed,' she told him coolly, 'but I still don't see why I should tell you about him.'

'Don't you?' he laughed. 'Perhaps this will explain it!' Gently, he took her face in his hands and touched her mouth lightly with his, the lips gently teasing, exploring. Tara's whole body suddenly exploded into melting pleasure. Without thinking she let go of the tiller.

In the chaotic moments that followed she was given a heaven-sent chance to pull herself together again. Ryan obviously thought she had done it deliberately, but it was his quick reactions that saved their heads from the sudden swing of the boom as the *Primavera* headed into the wind.

He took the rudder himself while Tara made good her escape. 'I see it's to be "hands off"!' he said with a quick, glinting smile. 'Don't worry, I've got the message—at least while we're out sailing,' he finished outrageously.

Shattered by her response, she decided it would be prudent to play it cool, so said nothing, just lay down on the tilting deck, letting the sun soak into her skin before it became too hot. She was quite aware of Ryan's interest though; she thought his eyes burned her body even more than the sun. Anyway, one thing had been made clear to her this morning. He wanted her quite as much as she wanted him, and whatever they thought about each other didn't seem to make the slightest difference to the sizzling sexual awareness that hung between them.

There were three other larger yachts already at anchor when they reached Po Toi Island and waited for the sampan to come and meet them. Ryan had to avoid the nets and the holding cages full of fish, so they had already dropped sail, and the *Primavera* swung lazily in the sea, the anchor holding her steady.

'Time for a swim before lunch, don't you think?' His eyes dared her to refuse, but she was in her element in the water, and agreed enthusiastically.

He dropped some steps over the stern, but Tara didn't wait. She dived effortlessly over the side, revelling in the smooth silky feel of the warm water on her body. He followed her quickly, just waiting to strip off his shorts to reveal swimming-trunks almost as lurid as her Ken Done outfit.

'Mind the nets, Tara! Swim out to sea rather than inland.'

She acknowledged his words, and struck out into a fast crawl, intensely happy, but he soon caught her up.

'You swim like a fish,' he told her admiringly, 'a mermaid, no less!'

She trod water opposite him. 'I've always loved it. I try to swim every day, but a pool is never the same, is it?'

He shook the water off his face, and Tara once more became far too aware of his powerful body, which the crystal-clear water did little to hide. She turned away again in a fast crawl, but he kept up with her.

'Don't go too far out!' he gasped. 'We won't have time for lunch at this rate.'

Obediently, she turned, and in a more leisurely way they both swam back to the boat. The steps made it easy for her to climb back on *Primavera*.

'A quick shower to wash off the salt, then we'll be ready. Look!' He pointed out the sampan already on its way out to them. She hurried, her tummy warning her that she was hungry after the morning at sea, and was back up on deck in time to hear him bargaining with the Chinese owner for the fee he wanted to charge to row them to the shore.

It was a relief in some ways to hear Ryan greeted by a number of friendly voices as they walked into the simple restaurant. They were all English or Australians, and it wasn't long before they were in the middle of a noisy, laughing group.

'So, you're Seb Halliday's daughter!' Shrewd eyes assessed her. 'I remember you when you were a little girl, but I don't suppose you remember me?'

Tara smiled then frowned a little in concentration as she studied the older man's face. 'I do know your face, but I can't remember your name. I'm probably wrong, but didn't you have something to do with racing?'

A delighted smile told her she'd hit base. 'What a memory! Yes, I train horses for your father, have done all these years.'

'Of course,' she gave her warm smile in return, 'you're Brian Bourne!'

'So what are you doing out here, Tara?'

'I've come to see Daddy, and to find myself a job.'

'Great stuff! You must come and have dinner soon. Isn't Seb away at the moment?'

'Yes, sadly he is, but he should be home in the next couple of days.'

Brian lowered his voice. 'The company's been having a bit of a problem. Seb's gone to the States to drum up a bit of financial support, as I expect you know. Shame, really; there's nothing wrong with Hall Bay, but like all the companies here they're trying to diversify their interests, and that Singapore deal has definitely left them with a short-term cash crisis, or so I gather. . . Seb hasn't bought any new horses this year.'

'Filling Tara in on all the local gossip?' Ryan's voice had a definite edge to it.

'Don't be so touchy, old boy!' Brian gave a grunt of laughter. 'She's family, and if she doesn't already know most of it it's about time she was told. It's been too long since she was out here with us all. I suppose that was your mother's fault?'

'How right you are!' Tara smiled at him warmly. 'Mummy couldn't believe anyone could be happy in Hong Kong for so long, so she kept me with her.'

'Silly woman,' Brian said, indulgently, 'but she was quite something to look at.' He allowed his eyes to rove over Tara before continuing, 'Luckily you've inherited her good looks, my dear.'

'Do you think so?' Tara looked surprised. Her mother had often moaned that she didn't look much like her.

'I didn't mean you look exactly like her; I meant that you have good looks.'

'That's more diplomatic than you usually are, Brian,' Ryan interrupted.

'Oh, I know I'm blunt. Call a spade a spade and all that. . . It's my Northern upbringing, I expect,'

Brian finished complacently, 'but I still know a beautiful woman when I see one!'

Tara, risking a quick look, saw that Ryan's face still wore a distinctly sardonic expression.

'Do you like horses, Ryan?' she ventured.

'Not much,' was the quick response. 'One end bites and the other end kicks. . .' He grinned at the outcry from most of the others at the tables around them. 'I agree they can be beautiful to look at, but that's it as far as I'm concerned.'

'Don't you like to gamble?' Tara continued to probe.

'He's no punter,' Brian jovially interrupted, 'minds too much if he loses!'

'There are many things I'm prepared to take a calculated gamble on, but to put your money on anything as unpredictable as a horse, and I mean serious money, has to be insanity.'

'The Chinese are great gamblers, aren't they?' Tara appealed.

'Indeed they are, and they're not known as inscrutable for nothing!'

Everyone laughed at Ryan, including Tara, because he pulled a silly face at her, and from that moment he took charge of the conversation, telling light-hearted jokes and generally keeping everyone in fits of laughter until he decided that it was time for them to leave.

Back once more on the *Primavera* Tara felt sleepy. Maybe it was that bottle of ice-cold wine that Ryan had taken to the restaurant with them in a cool-box, or maybe it was just too much sun and sea air. Whatever it was, once they were under way again she made no attempt to move away when Ryan came to sit next to her and took control of the tiller.

They talked, idly and companionably, about everything and nothing as the small yacht lifted them gracefully over the swell as they continued their way around the island, but it wasn't long before she drifted off into a light doze, then woke up disconcerted to find her head on Ryan's shoulder, and one arm holding her firmly against his warm body.

'Wake up, sleepy head! We've been on this tack far too long, but I didn't want to disturb you. Ready to go about!' They tacked their way past Big Wave Bay and up to Lei Yue Mun Channel. Tara could now see the great tongue of Kai Tak's landing-strip ahead of her. Her short sleep had completely revived her, so she was once more wide awake and interested.

'It's so sad that none of the junks have their beautiful sails now,' she mourned as they were passed by one of the modern engined equivalents. 'You used to see far more of them when I was little.'

'Yes, I suppose it is sad, and they were very picturesque, I agree, but from a convenience point of view—well, the modern junks are far more practical. You must come out on the company junk one day. It's a great deal easier to sunbathe on it, for one thing.'

'I suppose you prefer this yacht,' she said pertly.

'Of course,' he answered quietly, 'this is where I do my thinking. . .'

'I hope I haven't distracted you too much?' she queried with a smile.

'You know perfectly well that you have distracted me a great deal!' He took a quick look at her slightly crestfallen face. 'Very pleasurable it's been too.'

This made her laugh again, but soon they had to concentrate on the *Primavera* as they made their way through one of the busiest harbours in the world.

The sun was low in the sky when they tied up at the yacht club. 'We'll come back here for dinner, shall we?' Ryan queried. 'They do very good food—that is, if you're not too tired?'

'No, I'm fine now.' She smiled at him, then lowered her eyes in case he could see how happy she was that this day had not after all come to an end.

'Good. We'll stop off and change. If you're serious about not moving into your father's house, will you be happy to stay in the apartment?'

'If that's possible, then I'll be more than happy, always supposing I can pay the rent on my own!'

'I expect the company will take care of that.'

'No!' He turned to look at her, surprised at the violence of her reaction. 'If I can afford to live there, I will. If not, I'll move out and share like everyone else!'

He glanced at her sideways. 'It isn't easy to find reasonable accommodation anywhere in Hong Kong, unless you're prepared to move out to the new territories.

'I know! But I still prefer to pay my own way.'

'Well, you can argue with your father. He owns the whole block.' He glanced again at her rigid profile. 'Don't worry! He bought it before we joined forces.'

Tara was grateful that she didn't have to explain her actions, although judging by the expression on Ryan's face perhaps he had guessed part of her reasons anyway. At least he seemed to have got the message that she didn't intend to be beholden to him or anyone else, but it had certainly put a damper on the better relationship they seemed to have built up today. And maybe that was all to the good, she reminded herself, because it would be all too easy to forget her reservations about him when she was under the spell of his easy charm.

CHAPTER FOUR

TARA prowled restlessly around the sitting-room waiting for Ryan to come and pick her up—he was already twenty minutes late. Her grey silk dress shimmered and turned to silver as the light caught it, its soft folds moulding her body seductively. She couldn't help wondering what had delayed him.

She stopped by the big mirror and looked back at her reflection. Tonight she had striven for cool sophistication and she was pleased with her image. She had swept her hair up into a neat coil which showed off the beauty of her long neck and the bones of her face. Heavy blue crystal earrings hung long, framing her face. Clever use of make-up had emphasised her large tawny eyes and high cheekbones. She hoped she looked exotic and expensive enough to make Ryan pause if he thought he was just going to seduce a naïve young girl. Because after today she had no real doubts that that was his intention.

Whatever her own feelings were, she was going to make it more than clear that she was no push-over. It would do him good, she told herself, because she was fairly sure that most women fell like ninepins before his devastating charm.

When she heard the doorbell she collected her short silk jacket and bag before moving—she had no intention of inviting him in for a drink, particularly as he had kept her waiting so long.

She gave him a cool glance, ignoring the brooding expression on his face as his eyes took in her appearance in their usual comprehensive manner.

'I'm sorry I'm late—there have been a number of calls I've had to return.'

Tara allowed her brows to rise slightly, but she didn't answer, leaving the ball firmly in his court.

'Would you mind very much if we joined a party of businessmen this evening?' he asked her abruptly. 'That—er—acquaintance of yours, Brett Moncrieff, has set it up. He wants me to meet some people in connection with a deal Hall Bay could be interested in.'

She didn't attempt to conceal her surprise, but hoped the very real jolt of hearing Brett Moncrieff's name in connection with Hall Bay wasn't obvious to him. It came to her that now she had all the pieces of the puzzle firmly in place. Why hadn't she connected Brett with the take-over earlier? Now she knew exactly why she had been invited to Australia, and why Ryan hadn't been too happy to see them sitting together in the bar at the Mandarin. 'No, I wouldn't mind at all, but——' she allowed her voice to sound faintly sarcastic '—— I can quite easily make alternative arrangements if that would suit you better?'

'No, it would not!' he answered explosively.

'And if you're going to be working for me in the near future, then this is the kind of thing you're going to have to get used to. Come on, let's go! We've wasted enough time already as I get the message that I'm not going to be invited in and given a drink.'

She had the grace to look a little ashamed, but not for long—her mind was too busy trying to put two and two together, working out how Brett and Ryan had got together in the first place and why he should want to kick her father out of Hall Bay.

Brett was part of a rather loud and noisy group at the bar when they joined him, and he showed no particular signs of wanting to stop being the life and soul of the party even after their arrival. Tara began to resent being treated as an outsider, even though she was the only woman, and she disliked the slightly knowing looks in the eyes of some of the men. Ryan had been quickly absorbed into the group, and after a casual introduction of her seemed quite happy to ignore her also. It was with relief that she caught the eye of a friend who was sitting alone at a small table, obviously waiting for his guests for the evening. Unhurriedly she moved over to talk to him, prolonging the conversation as long as she could to avoid having to return to Brett and Ryan, but she wasn't left alone for long.

'Sorry about that, Tamara! Got to keep the boys happy though.' Brett acknowledged her companion with a brief nod, before expertly piloting her away towards another table where Ryan was already seated with two Chinese men. The Australian studied her carefully. 'You look great! Sorry again about ignoring you, but I've got my reputation to think of, as well as yours.'

'Then why include me in this dinner?' She resisted the pressure of his arm on her elbow, stopping to study the pleasant face bent close to hers. He looked about as cuddly as a teddy-bear if you ignored the steel-sharp eyes.

'Oh, come on, now! Neither Ryan nor I would want to stand up a pretty girl.' A quick glance from narrowed eyes was enough to inform him that she wasn't going to be soothed so easily. 'All right! Marcel Chang's sitting at that table with Ryan. He's chairman of the biggest bank in Asia, and, as he was supposed to marry your stepmother until she decided otherwise, he wants to meet you.'

'Wants to meet me?' Tara couldn't hide her surprise.

'Apparently he used to see you when you were a child. Play it sweet, Tamara, and I promise you you'll find it worth your while.' Without giving her a chance to protest further, he propelled her onwards, ignoring her reluctance, to where the others, now on their feet, were ready to welcome her.

Long years of training at her mother's house made sure her manners were perfect, but she wasn't at all sure about the sardonic expression on

Ryan's face as he watched her reply to Marcel
Chang's query.

'I've wanted to come back to Hong Kong for a
long time,' she murmured, quietly amazed at the
bottle of champagne which was brought over to
them, accompanied by a couple of 'tinnies' of
Australian beer. She wasn't sure she remembered
Marcel, but she had never had any problem in
getting on with the Chinese, and he appeared a
charming and gentle man who it was a pleasure to
talk to. Deliberately she shut Ryan and Brett Moncrieff out of her mind, and her success was assured
when she began slowly to talk to Marcel in
Cantonese.

The absolute amazement on Ryan's and Brett's
faces gave her great pleasure, and when it became
clear, as it soon did, that Ryan's Chinese did not
extend to more than a few phrases, then for the
first time that evening she began to relax. Inevitably the party split into those willing to talk
Cantonese and the two others who could not.

Tara soon found herself being asked a number
of oblique questions about Brett Moncrieff and his
connection with her, which she found difficult to
answer, although she did her best to appear
unconcerned. He talked about her father very
kindly as well, making it clear he counted him a
friend, which she found encouraging, particularly
after Brett's mention of her stepmother.

All the time though she was intensely conscious
of the other two. She became increasingly aware

of Brett's frustration although his feelings were not allowed to show on the bland, smiling face. Ryan, after his initial shock, seemed to spend the whole evening watching her closely, although his face also gave little away. It seemed to her that he inaugurated little conversation, leaving Brett to make all the effort of appearing perfectly happy with the way things had turned out.

It was Mr Chang who at the end of the dinner reverted to talking English again, and the conversation became more business-orientated. Tara was happy by now to take a back seat as she watched Brett move into action; anyway, she was far more interested in Ryan's reaction to it all, but it seemed that he intended to keep his thoughts to himself. If she hadn't known how things were between them she would have been surprised at how aloof he kept himself from the proposed deal. He didn't seem to be giving Brett any active encouragement at all, and more than once she noticed surprise in Mr Chang's eyes at his lack of response to Brett's enthusiasm.

It was Ryan who broke up the party as well, sweeping her away with fluid excuses about how tired she must be, without giving her a chance to protest, and totally ignoring Brett's obvious dislike of his high-handedness. When they were alone in the taxi she decided to tackle him about it.

'Well! I wouldn't have thought that had to be one of your most successful evenings. I thought

you were supposed to be interested in the deal?'
she queried.

'Not really.' His voice sounded lazy and a little
bored. 'Moncrieff leant on me a bit. I think he
really wanted to be sure you came along. I wonder
why?'

She heard the question in his voice and wasn't
fooled by his relaxed manner, so was on her guard.
'Because Mr Chang remembered me as a child
apparently and wanted to meet me again.' Her
voice sounded light and casual as she continued,
'He's a charming man, isn't he? And a great friend
of my father's, I gather——'

'Not that great a friend,' Ryan interrupted.
'Don't forget he lost considerable face when Serena
chose not to marry him——'

'Nonsense!' It was her turn to interrupt. 'I don't
think that worries him one little bit. We were
talking about it at dinner!'

'Yes, so I gathered. . .'

She turned a shocked face towards him. 'But
you don't speak Cantonese!'

'That doesn't mean that I don't understand it!
Which reminds me. Where did you learn to speak
so fluently?'

'When I was a child over here, but I expect I
would have forgotten most of it if I hadn't found
someone to practise with in the holidays at home.'

'I can see that I am going to have to watch my
step with you, but there's no denying that it's
going to be a very useful accomplishment when

you start work at Hall Bay.' He picked up one of her hands and swung it lightly. 'Which reminds me—how soon can you start work?'

'I—well, I don't know. . . I thought perhaps after Daddy comes home?'

'Great! That means you can start on Monday. I'll give you a lift into work each day.'

'Now wait a minute! I thought I was supposed to have a holiday first?'

She caught a glimpse of white teeth as he smiled. 'I need you at Hall Bay, Tara. If you're not prepared to start then, I'll have to look for someone else.' His hold on her hand tightened painfully.

'Blackmail?' she queried sweetly.

'If that's the way you choose to look at it, maybe, but I prefer to think of it as an answer to my problem of finding a new assistant!'

The taxi stopped outside a brightly lit doorway and Ryan gave a low laugh at her bewildered expression. 'You didn't really think I was going to let the evening end there, did you? This is Hong Kong's latest and, I'm told, hottest spot in town. Come on, out you get! I've just endured an appallingly boring evening, and now I want to have fun!' Quite unable to resist his laughing charm, she grinned and allowed him to lead her through the doorway towards the insistent sounds of the latest chart-toppers.

Back in her room later, Tara had to admit that he was an extremely entertaining companion. She wasn't going to lose sight of the fact that her only real interest to him was her shares in Hall Bay, although he was clever enough to try to make her forget it. He was a superb dancer, and Tara decided that the only thing to do was to live for the minute. After all, the day had been a success, and Ryan hadn't even attempted to lay a finger on her as he'd dropped her at the door of her flat. Although she'd had every intention of putting him in his place if he'd attempted to kiss her again, it was still irritating that he didn't even try, and she was fairly sure he'd guessed her thoughts pretty accurately as well because of the amusement in his eyes as he had left her.

She wished she weren't so ambivalent in her feelings about him. At a primitive level she had no doubts at all. He was the most entertaining and charming man she had ever met, yet at the same time she was at perpetual war with herself. Instinct warned her that he mistrusted her almost as much she questioned his every move.

If he was working with Brett Moncrieff, then he was going to extraordinary and unusual lengths to try and put distance between them. Because of her heightened awareness as far as he was concerned she knew he was abnormally interested in how close a friend Brett Moncrieff really was of hers. She had the vague idea that the only reason he had agreed to the dinner in the first place was to see exactly how friendly they were, which, as she told herself, was absurd. Both of them were only interested in her share of Hall Bay, on which depressing thought she firmly made herself go to sleep.

She was on the point of leaving the apartment the next morning when she was delayed by a messenger. He handed her a small parcel, making her sign a receipt, before leaving. Curious, she opened it to find an exquisitely carved piece of jade. It was of a tiny deer, resting under the shade of a tree.

Gently she ran her fingers over it, delighting in the smooth feel of the stone and the delicacy of the carving before her brows drew together in a frown. She was no expert, far from it, but she knew enough to know that it was worth a great deal of money. Carefully she put it down on the low table in front of her, then began to search for a card, but there was nothing.

The phone rang and absently she picked it up.

'Yes?'

'I have a call for Miss Hall.'

'Speaking.'

'One moment, Miss Hall, I'm putting you through.'

'Good morning, Tamara. I hope you like your present?'

'Brett!' she gasped. 'Why on earth——'

I promised I'd make it worth your while if you joined us for dinner, didn't I?'

'For heaven's sake! I didn't expect anything, let alone something as beautiful and valuable——'

'Glad you like it, I rather hoped you would.'

'Well, of course, it's beautiful.' Tara took a deep breath. 'Look, Brett, I can't possible accept it.'

'Why not? You more than earned it. Marcel Chang is a difficult chap to get to meet, even for me!' She heard his laugh. 'Anyway, your nattering away in Chinese obviously did the trick because I think we're going to be able to interest him in our plans after all.'

'But that was nothing to do with me!' Tara tried to sort out her tangled thoughts. Rich businessmen did not hand out valuable presents to anyone without expecting something in exchange, and she had a nasty feeling that she was somehow being set up. Nothing she had said or done last night could possibly warrant such an extravagant gesture. 'Anyway, I'm sorry, Brett. It was a very kind idea, but there's no way I can possibly keep it!'

It seemed that he heard and took note of the firm conviction in her voice because as she braced herself for renewed pressure he gave an exaggerated sigh. 'OK, but I'll give it to you one day, even if it has to be your wedding present! There is one more condition, though, and that's that you spend the afternoon with me at Happy Valley. I'm off back home this evening.'

Relieved and absurdly grateful that he accepted her decision so gracefully, and was on the point of leaving, she accepted more warmly than she would have thought possible a couple of minutes ago. 'Yes, I'd love to do that.'

'Great. I'm sorry I can't give you lunch, but I'll pick you up at your apartment, shall I?'

This was going too far. 'No. I'll meet you at the Mandarin. I'm already lunching quite near.'

'Can you make it by two-thirty?' He waited for her affirmative before ringing off.

Tara wondered what she had let herself in for, then shrugged her shoulders. Nothing much could happen to her on the racetrack, and she'd always loved horse-racing, like her father.

Brett greeted her in his usual boisterous manner, hustling her out to the car as if every minute was precious and not to be wasted in small talk. He took the small package that she had so carefully wrapped and put it into one of his pockets with no comment, except to give her a quick smile.

'I'm looking forward to the racing, it's been a long time since I've been to Happy Valley,' she told him enthusiastically, hoping her change of subject would make sure he didn't mention the jade carving.

Brett turned to look at her in astonishment. 'I'm not going to the racecourse! I'm going to look at the Tiger Balm Gardens. I want to see first hand what the Chinese want in the way of entertainment. I thought you would realise after last night!'

'The Tiger Balm Gardens?' It was Tara's turn to look amazed. She opened her mouth to protest, then shut it again, unable to think of anything to say.

Brett laughed. 'I gather their taste is a bit of a

shock to Westerners, but when China opens her doors to us I want to be ready to grab a piece of the action, and amusement parks are big business nowadays.' He laughed again. 'I've heard it described as a hallucinogenic Chinese Disneyland, and I'm intrigued!'

Tara remembered the gardens from her childhood, when her amah had taken her there. It had been a mad, zany sight even then, with terraced grottos full of bizarre stone sculptures from the most awful tales of Chinese mythology. Ostentatious, gaudy, even as a child she'd found little attractive about it, yet it was immensely popular with the Chinese.

'If I'd known where you were going, I'd have let you come alone!' she protested.

'Don't be such a spoil-sport! It can't be that bad——'

'You haven't seen it,' she interrupted him. 'Anyway, I can't think why you wanted me to come with you.'

'The pleasure of your company of course.' He gave her a quick smile. 'I always like to combine business with pleasure if I possibly can!'

Tara was forced to laugh, but she didn't protest any more as he took her arm and led her into what she privately thought was a psychedelic nightmare. In fact walking around with Brett was something of an education. He seemed able to ignore the garish splendour that surrounded them, or at least look at it with a critical, businesslike eye.

'I can't see us ever having the designers to cope with this!' he ended up saying with amusement after an exhaustive tour of the attractions offered. 'I think it will definitely take a Chinese mind to come up with the right ideas, don't you agree?'

'You're so right,' she agreed. 'Now can we go?'

He looked a little crestfallen. 'I'm sorry, Tamara, this really was a crazy idea of mine, but I wanted your company, so. . .' He shrugged his shoulders ruefully, and looked around him. 'Hey, look! You can have your fortune told here. . .'

'So we can, and almost certainly in Chinese, which means you won't understand a word of it.'

'I was thinking of you.'

Slightly disconcerted she protested, 'I wouldn't have thought you were the type to believe in fortune-tellers!'

'Ah, but you're wrong. I was told as a young boy that I'd make a lot of money, and now look at me!'

Tara smiled at his sudden sincerity. 'I'd say that was all by your own efforts.'

'Maybe, yes, but it helped me to believe I would be successful.' He took a handful of notes from his wallet and pushed her into the grotto. 'Let's see what they can predict of your future!'

Tara found herself standing alone in the dimly lit cave except for a small boy, who took her hand and led her further into the gloom towards a low bamboo chair set in front of a small table covered in lurid, swirling designs.

'Sit, please,' the child told her in lisping, accented Cantonese. After she had obeyed him, he left her to disappear even further into the darkness of the back of the cave.

An ancient Chinese man came forward, dressed in old-fashioned flowing robes, and knelt before the table. Speaking in sing-song fashion, he told her to lay her hands on the table, the palms facing upwards. He then drew out a pouch, and, opening it, threw some curiously shaped stones on to the table.

There was a heavy silence as he studied her hands, then the pattern the stones had made as they fell from his hand. His voice was full of the quavering tones of the very old as he began to speak, and Tara had difficulty at first in understanding him. He told her of her life to date, and of her parents' divorce, and in spite of herself she began to be impressed.

'When the moon wears the coat of the tiger, beware of he who hunts in its light. He will have the power to tear the heart from your breast. Danger is stalking you through the darkness of the night, and there is no way you can escape unless you return to the West, very soon.'

The voice stopped, and silently the old man withdrew into the deeper shadows. It was the child tugging at her dress who brought her back to reality.

She put the notes Brett had given her into the

outstretched hand of the child and silently followed him out into the garish reality of the Tiger Balm Gardens.

'Hey, you look a bit dazed! Did you learn anything exciting?' Brett took her arm possessively and began walking them both back towards the car.

Tara fought to make what she had just heard into something commonplace. 'Not really. It was all wrapped up in pretty phrases, fairly meaningless, but he seemed to know about my parents' divorce.'

'Write it all down before you forget it, Tamara. Who knows, on thinking about it you might be able to unravel a few clues as to what it all meant?'

'Thanks for the advice, but I don't think I'll bother. After all, I don't believe in fortune-tellers!'

He gave her a sharp look, but didn't say any more until they were back at the car. 'John wants me to tell you that he's made everything all right with your mother, by the way. You can go home whenever you like, but he's bought a small house for you just in case. . .' He caught her off guard then, and she found it impossible to hide all her emotions. He didn't seem to expect her to answer, just handed her an envelope with her name on it. She recognised her stepfather's writing, and without opening it put it in her bag.

The blue eyes had a quizzical expression in them as he took in her expression. 'Ah, well, I thought not, particularly as your father hasn't returned yet.

Don't feel you have to stay out here if it doesn't work out. If you find you need a change of air you'll be more than welcome in Perth.'

'Thanks, Brett! I'm sorry but as I've only just arrived back in Hong Kong I don't want to leave quite yet. Anyway, thanks for acting as postman. You can pass back a message that I'm fine.'

'Sure, I understand. Now, I've got to get back to do some business. Is there anywhere you'd like to be dropped?'

'No, thanks. I'll take a taxi, and thank you again for passing on John's message.'

'No trouble! Well, don't go and do something crazy, like falling in love.' His eyes, now hard again, did their best to pierce the armour of her secret thoughts, but Tara was on guard and returned his look with smiling guilelessness as she met his probing gaze.

'Thanks for the dinner, and this afternoon's entertainment.'

'Sure you're happy to be left here?'

'Quite sure.' She smiled back, and watched as he got into the car and was driven away, but her smile disappeared as soon as he had gone. She had a nasty suspicious mind, maybe, but she couldn't rid herself of the suspicion that this afternoon she had walked into another neat trap set up by Brett Moncrieff. That fortune-teller in the Tiger Balm Gardens was just a little bit too much of a coincidence for her to swallow. Particularly with his lurid advice about returning to the West as soon as possible because of danger. She smiled to herself as she remembered what he had told her about the moon wearing the coat of a tiger, for heaven's sake! Still thinking about the afternoon, she frowned as she considered again Brett Moncrieff.

He'd handled the whole afternoon very cleverly, but perhaps not quite cleverly enough. Deep in thought she began to walk slowly down Tai Hang Road, too busy with her thoughts to take one of the many taxis cruising hopefully past her, too busy indeed even to read the letter from her stepfather.

She was shaken out of her thoughts by Ryan's voice. 'Want a lift, Tamara?' He gestured back at a taxi parked just behind them.

'You? What on earth are you doing in this part of the town?' Surprise and shock made her sound unintentionally aggressive.

'Following you, of course, what else?' There was an edge behind the hardness of his words and she noticed with widened eyes that he was in a temper. Hard hands pushed her towards the waiting taxi.

'Hey! Now, wait a minute. . .' she started to protest, but his superior strength brooked no argument, and she found herself uncomfortably seated on the back seat before she had time to catch her breath. Cross, she tried to straighten her skirt and move away from his hard body, which was pressed disturbingly close to hers. She began to feel extremely uncomfortable, and her breathing quickened as she saw the anger in his face. 'What on earth's the matter?' Her voice sounded high and a little scared, and she tried to regain at least some measure of poise as she pushed her dishevelled hair away from her face.

'We've just had some bad news about your father. He's in hospital in the States. A suspected heart attack,' he told her bluntly. For a moment she thought he was going to hit her, because the blue eyes looked murderous. Bewildered tears filled her own eyes at the lack of pity on his face.

'How serious is it?' she half whispered. It took all her courage to ask that question because she was so frightened of his answer.

'Luckily for you this time it's more of a warning than anything else.' The hard eyes still blazed with fury. 'But if you go on having assignations with Moncrieff, who's just about the biggest shark ever to swim out of Australian waters, you'll probably kill him!'

'If I go on. . .' The implication of what he had just said suddenly clicked in her brain. Fury as great as his own, fuelled by her worry, swelled inside her. Without her even consciously thinking about it, one hand connected sharply with his cheek. 'How dare you speak to me like that——?' she began, but she was given no chance to finish. Ryan pulled her savagely into his arms, his mouth claiming hers with furious passion.

She tried to fight him off, but her struggles

became weaker as her body succumbed to the devastation of her senses. When he finally released her she lay back against the seat quite incapable of speaking, all the nerve-ends in her body alive and twitching in response to his savage kiss.

His voice sounded slurred as he looked into her enormous eyes. 'You've been asking for that ever since we first met, so don't expect me to apologise!'

She noticed the driver's eyes in his mirror avidly watching her reactions to the furious man next to her, as she tried desperately to pull herself together.

'I'm taking you to Serena. She wants to see you before she leaves for the States, although God knows why!'

Tara noticed that he seemed to have regained control of himself a great deal sooner than she had, but that helped her to remember what had gone before. Slowly and deliberately she opened her bag, and taking out a tissue began to wipe her lips fastidiously before crumpling it in her hand to throw it away. She allowed her eyes to meet his and saw with pleasure that her gesture had brought a dull flush to his cheeks.

Her mouth felt full and swollen but she had no intention of putting on more make-up to hide what had happened. Pain at hearing about her father was mixed with the disgust she felt at herself for responding to that kiss. She desperately wanted a shower, as if by washing her body she could wash away her instinctive response to the man sitting next to her.

CHAPTER FIVE

TARA made absolutely no attempt to talk to Ryan as the taxi slowly made its way through the traffic and up The Peak towards her father's house. What indeed could she have said to him after the way she had responded to his kiss? She guessed he was far too experienced a man not to have known what he had done to her and she was bitterly ashamed of her response. She forced her mind to concentrate instead on her father and the worrying news about him.

From what Ryan had said it seemed that he had been reporting her movements to her father— spying on her, in fact. Again her mind leapt away in fury until with an almost supreme effort of will she forced her thoughts back. Whatever Ryan said, she knew that her father trusted her, so it had to be something else that was worrying him, and that had to be the company.

When the taxi drew up in front of the familiar door Tara was out of it almost before it had stopped moving. Serena was standing there waiting for them, and Tara ran towards her. 'Any more news?' she called out breathlessly to the tiny but supremely elegant lady waiting to greet her with open arms.

'No, darling, but in this case no news is good news. Ryan did tell you that it wasn't serious?' As Tara bent her face to give her a kiss Serena suddenly frowned as she noticed the girl's swollen lips. 'Tara! Are you all right, my dear? What has happened?' A gentle finger just lightly touched her mouth, and she looked over the girl's shoulder to Ryan, who was still paying the taxi driver.

Tara's eyes blazed with rage, and her stepmother took a step back, her whole attitude one of astonishment. 'No, I can't believe. . . It wasn't Ryan who did that to you?'

'Oh, yes, it was! Forget it, Serena, it isn't important, I'll tell you about it later. Now I want to hear about Daddy.' There was a still an expression of surprise on her stepmother's face and also worry, but she gave Tara a sweet smile.

'There's nothing terribly urgent to tell you. He's absolutely fine and longing to come home, but the doctors are keeping him quiet for a week. They've done an ECG and no particular problem has shown up.' She saw Ryan walking towards them as the taxi turned in the drive to leave. 'Why don't you go up to your room, my dear? Everything is ready for you and we'll talk later, when we're alone.'

Tara realised that the last thing she wanted to face at the moment was Ryan trying to excuse himself to Serena, and as the news about Daddy didn't seem too bad she half smiled at her stepmother, and walked quickly into the house.

'Tara, wait!' She heard Ryan's voice, but didn't stop as she ran up the shallow stairs. Serena would make sure he didn't follow her, but if he dared to come upstairs—well, her room had a lock and key which she wouldn't hesitate to use.

She made straight for the adjoining bathroom without bothering to give her old room more than a cursory glance. The mirror showed her swollen lips and it was all too obvious that she had been violently kissed. She made a moue of distaste before soaking some tissues in cold water to make a compress to reduce the swelling. Holding them against her face, she wandered back into what used to be her bedroom, and, looking around her, her childhood.

Her eyes were soon shining with unshed tears as she saw how little had been changed. All her favourite books were still in the bookcase and the toy chest was full of old-remembered favourites.

Serena found her there, on her knees, surrounded by an ever-growing pile of half-forgotten memories, and she gave her stepdaughter a smile. 'I'd have thought you were a little too big for those things now, Tara!'

'Oh, Serena! I never thought. . . You know Mummy wouldn't let me take much with me when we left. I never guessed you would have kept all these things!'

'You can thank your father, not me. It was his idea that if you ever returned you would find everything exactly as you left it.'

Tara's eyes filled with tears. 'Will he really be all right?'

'Of course he will!'

If Tara thought her stepmother spoke a little too firmly, as if she was trying to convince herself, then she didn't say so. She just smiled and slowly stood up.

'I expect you think I'm mad——' she gestured with one hand at the clutter all around her '—but I couldn't resist seeing if they were all there.'

'No, not mad exactly,' Serena laughed, 'just a little cracked, that's all! Now come downstairs and have some tea with me. I think that would be better for you than playing with your old toys. Ryan's gone so we won't be disturbed.'

Tara flushed as she noticed Serena looking at her lips. 'Give me a minute to tidy myself and I'll be right with you.'

'No—you look fine as you are. Don't worry Tara, the swelling has gone down, and I want to hear exactly what happened between you two.'

Kicking off her shoes, Tara curled up on the big sofa next to Serena. She kept her eyes firmly on the cup of delicately scented tea as she told her what had happened that afternoon. 'You see,' she ended up saying, 'Ryan has never trusted me, right from the start. He thinks I'm going to sell my shares in Hall Bay to Brett Moncrieff, if I haven't already done so.'

'Yes, I'm very sorry about that, Tara, and I know Seb will be angry as well. But why did he kiss you?

I think he must be very attracted to you to have behaved to badly!' She smiled a little mischievously at the girl sitting next to her. 'He is very sorry for what happened. . .' But Tara kept her face impassive. 'I hope you will forgive him, my dear? He has promised me never to let it happen again. I think this has been quite a shock for him, because normally he is the one who has to fight the girls off!' She waited to see if Tara was going to react before continuing. 'I blame myself, of course. I should have been here to welcome you when you arrived.'

'Oh, no!' Tara protested. 'Why should you? It was such a spur of the moment decision, and truly I've been fine.'

'Still, while I'm away, and until your father gets back, will you live here, please? I shall feel much happier to think of you here in your own home.'

'Serena!' Tara took hold of her stepmother's hands. 'This is your home now, not mine. I'm not going to live here, playing gooseberry between the two of you.'

There was a small silence as the two women looked at each other. 'You are a very kind girl, Tara, and a very understanding one as well, but as far as I am concerned you must always look on this place as your home.'

Tara suddenly grinned. 'Oh, no, stepmamma! You are far too pretty for me to bring my boy-friends back here safely. I think I would prefer to go on living in the flat. But, if it will make you happy, I'll move in here until you and Daddy come back. OK?'

Serena gently squeezed her hands. 'If that's what you wish. . . But your father may think differently.'

'No, he won't,' Tara replied confidently. 'If he's going to see me at work all day then the last thing he'll want is me here as well.'

Serena gave a little sigh. 'Your father has been thinking of retiring, leaving Ryan to run the company. He would like to be chairman perhaps. You see, his doctor has warned him to slow down, so this minor heart attack has not been too much of a surprise for me. I feared it could happen, and so did Ryan, particularly when there has been such a run on the shares. I know Seb feared a take-over, which is why he's gone to the States. He needed to negotiate a substantial loan to make sure Hall Bay was safe. Luckily he managed to do so before he was taken ill, which means his greatest worry has been taken away, so he should recover pretty quickly now he knows the company is safe.'

Tara looked worried. 'You're sure he's OK?'

'Yes, quite sure now. But I think it will be better for him to retire quickly, don't you?'

'If you can make him,' his daughter answered quickly.

'He has already agreed in principle. There is a lot of travelling we would like to do. Up to now he's been so busy at Hall Bay that there was never time, but I think he'll quite enjoy having more leisure. There is his golf, and also his horses. He knows a great deal about breeding, and I think would like to own a small stud, so you see there will be no lack of interests.'

'And I think you'll have to be careful that he doesn't work even harder than he does now!'

Serena laughed. 'Don't worry! I'll be there all the time to make sure that he doesn't. Now, I have to leave for the airport in half an hour. You will be all right here on your own?'

'Of course I will. Anyway, I'm hardly alone with all the servants, am I? I'll come with you to the airport.'

'No, I think it would be better if you didn't. You see, Ryan has insisted on accompanying me. I gather he has some papers that your father should see.'

'In that case I quite agree! I've had enough of Veryan Bay for one day, thank you.'

'You do not find him attractive?' Serena enquired a little provocatively.

Tara shot her a keen look before replying, 'I can see the attraction, yes, but I don't happen to like that kind of man. He thinks far too much of himself as far as women are concerned. It's about time someone put him in his place!'

Serena laughed. 'Perhaps that "someone" had better be you. Now I must go and change and check that Flora has packed everything for me. Don't worry, Tara, we'll keep in close touch.' She leant over to kiss her stepdaughter. 'There is perhaps just one thing that I know will fuss your father if the answer is "no". Can I tell him that you will be starting work for Hall Bay on Monday?'

The navy blue linen dress with the line of buttons through looked sufficiently businesslike and severe, Tara thought, even if it couldn't remotely be described as high fashion. She was disconcerted therefore in walking into Hall Bay's prestigious offices to discover that most of the female staff were wearing trendy clothes. Mini-skirts were everywhere, even if teamed with soft silk blouses suitable for day wear. There were some outfits that had her blinking in surprise as she realised that these were in advance of what was being sold in the shops in London—copies, in fact, of the very latest fashion design. Filing this away for future reference, she realised thankfully that more of her current wardrobe was going to be useful than she had thought. Used to the rather severe lines of what successful businesswomen wore in the city of London, she was encouraged until she heard the unmistakable voice of Ryan Bay. He was chatting up one of the younger girls, whose tight black leather mini was almost showing more of her legs than was decent as she sat in front of her computer console.

Tara hadn't seen or heard from him since their last, disastrous meeting, and she couldn't help her lips thinning as she saw the blatant way he was studying the leg-show in front of him. She wasn't in the least surprised to see that the girl was obviously enjoying every minute of his attention as she turned away to follow the young Chinese boy who had been delegated to show her her new office.

This, though small, was more than adequate, dominated by a large, modern desk with its computer and printer. She was surprised to notice a large vase full of what looked like several dozen long-stemmed red roses. She paused to admire the velvety texture of the petals, but knew better than to expect them to smell.

'Good morning, Tamara. I'm pleased you like the flowers. They're by the way of being a peace-offering as well as a welcome to your new job!' Ryan was leaning casually against the door-frame watching her with wary eyes.

She couldn't help her whole body stiffening in shock; she hadn't expected him to follow her quite so quickly. She also found it easier not to meet his eyes. 'Good morning, Ryan.' It ought to have been a simple job to say those three words, but her voice sounded husky and a little unsure even to her own ears. Irritated with herself, she cleared her throat, quite determined not to thank him for the flowers.

'I do hope you haven't caught a cold?' The concern she heard in the deep voice unnerved her for a moment although she was fairly sure it wasn't genuine. Ryan had an actor's gift of being able to use his voice to express any emotion he chose.

'No, I haven't!' she snapped back in a hurry, unwilling to elaborate.

'Good,' he returned smoothly, 'because there's a great deal of basic stuff you'll need to learn before you're going to be of the slightest use to me.' He tossed a couple of floppy disks on to her desk. 'Do you know how to work the computer?'

She took the opportunity to move further away from him, putting the barrier of the desk between them. 'Yes, I'm familiar with this model.'

'Right, I'll leave you to get on with it, then. I'm afraid you'll find there's a lot to read up as well.' He gestured to the pile of files on one side of the desk. 'When you've got through all that lot, and digested it, then we'll get together and see if you've got any ideas we might use.' He looked at her expression. 'Don't panic! I know there's a good week's work in front of you. I hope I don't have to say that everything you learn here is confidential?'

This gave her the courage to behave like herself. 'No, Ryan, you don't have to tell me that.' This time she met his eyes, squaring her chin in an unspoken challenge. There was an expression on his face that she found hard to read.

His lips moved into a smile that didn't reach his eyes. 'Seb and Serena seem to think that I have misjudged you; if I have I apologise, but if you're honest you'll admit that I had good reason to mistrust you.'

Her eyes narrowed as she responded sharply, 'And I have just as much reason to distrust you! It's been your expansionist plans that have got Hall Bay into this mess. For all I know you could be planning to ditch my father and throw in your hand with Moncrieff! You were the one who made sure I had dinner with him, after all.'

'Now why would I want to do that?' he demanded softly.

'Many people have lost confidence in the future of Hong Kong after the troubles in China,' she snapped. 'Why should I find it difficult to believe that you are one of them?'

'Because I told you quite the opposite on the way back from the airport, if you remember.'

'You might not have been telling the truth!'

'True. Just as you might right now be planning Hall Bay's downfall.'

'This is a stupid conversation,' she answered coldly, 'I suggest you take my father's word for it and leave me to get on with my work.'

'What was in that envelope Moncrieff handed you just before he left?'

Tara's face suddenly flamed with colour and she bit hard on her lower lip to stop herself losing her temper. She debated within herself whether to tell him or not, but decided there was nothing wrong with the truth. 'It was a letter from my stepfather, John Chacewater. He wrote to tell me that he's bought a small mews house for me. If I want to return to London, then that will be my home in the future.' She spoke coldly, unwilling to elaborate further.

'Do you know that Chacewater's have considerable investments in Moncrieff's business empire?'

Tara shrugged her shoulders. 'So what? Even you must admit that as one of the largest banks in America that must be a tiny fraction of their business!'

'So you don't accept that they have an interest in seeing Moncrieff's take-over bid for us succeed?'

'No, I don't! If you're as well-informed as you pretend, you should know that the Chacewater investment with Moncrieff's companies is only concerned with the marketing abroad of Australian wines.'

Ryan frowned at her heavily. 'You've discussed this company with your stepfather?'

Tara raised her eyebrows. 'You mean Hall Bay?'

'Yes.'

She shook her head. 'No, it isn't really a big enough concern; anyway, it's outside his field of interest.'

'Even though he's married the ex-wife. . .?'

'Even though,' she replied firmly.

He looked disbelieving but Tara had had enough of the conversation. Rather pointedly she sat down at the desk and pulled the nearest folder towards her, but he still didn't take the hint. She gave an exaggerated sigh when she looked up to find him still watching her under frowning brows. 'Look, Ryan! If I had ever really contemplated selling out my shares in Hall Bay do you really think I'd have bothered to come out here at all? I could have got rid of them just as easily in London.'

He gave her an enigmatic look, then shattered her by completely changing the subject. 'You've no need to dress like a nun just because you've come to work here. You aren't the only pretty girl in Hong Kong, you know, and I've never needed to push my way in where I wasn't invited.' He left then, giving her a self-satisfied smile, obviously delighted at having had the last word.

If looks could kill, then he'd have been dead before he walked out of the door, but Tara was left fuming, trying to think of something sufficiently cutting that would really have put him in his place.

Ryan's provocative last words severely strained her attention initially as she tried to concentrate on the mountain of reading she had to do, but luckily she was so interested in the subject that she soon managed to put him out of her mind. She didn't even leave her desk at lunchtime, preferring just to have a sandwich sent in to her. She was unaware that twice Ryan came to see how she was doing, so concentrated on her work that even his presence at her door failed to distract her.

It was Ryan also who called a halt, a good hour after most of the other staff had left. 'That's enough, Tara! It's time you went home.' Wearily she looked up then, her eyes meeting his with momentary shock. His voice sounded rough as he continued, 'You're not going to earn Brownie points from me if you try to cram a week's work in a couple of days. You've been at this desk all day without a break—now it's time you went home.'

'But I haven't finished reading this file!' she protested, bending her head once more. 'Anyway, I can find my own way home.'

'You might be prepared to sit here all night, but I've got other plans for the evening. Those folders are going back into the safe in my office where they belong—now! And they're not going to be released again to you until tomorrow morning. You've read more than enough for one day.'

Tara gave him a resentful look as he firmly shut the file she was reading, collecting the others she had already seen. 'Bring the rest into my office, will you?' he called over his shoulder as he left her.

She was conscious of an aching stiffness in her neck and shoulders as she stood up. He was quite right, of course; she had read so much that her head was spinning with figures, but that didn't stop her from feeling irritated and cross at being interrupted in her work. Slowly she followed him into the large room next to hers that was dominated by an enormous modern desk made of black slate. The safe was built into the wall, but she wasn't given a chance to see what was in it as Ryan's body screened the interior from her view.

She allowed her eyes to move rather scornfully around the room. There were a couple of sailing pictures, but otherwise it appeared strictly functional and modernistic. This was a room for working in, it seemed, with no trace of any sybaritic luxury that she had seen in other offices.

'Well? Do you like it?' Ryan's amused voice brought her sharply back to the present.

'Not particularly. All work and no play, you know. . .' She deliberately left the sentence unfinished.

He laughed. 'That's the way I like it! I've never believed in mixing business with pleasure. Work hard, play hard, that's my motto, and in that order. Remember that, Tara, and we should get on, but don't ever try to confuse the issue. When you walk into this room, it's business only, OK?'

'You are, without a doubt, the most arrogant man I've ever had the misfortune to meet!' she answered through gritted teeth. 'As far as I'm concerned the only relationship we have is strictly business, in office hours and out of it!'

'Now there's a provocative statement,' he cut in swiftly. 'I never refuse a challenge, Tara. . .' He gave her a long look that brought the blood rushing to her face. He moved nearer to her, and in panic she stepped back, knocking over a chair. 'Retreating already?' he mocked softly.

Picking up the chair gave her a chance to recover. 'It's business only in this room, Ryan. Remember your rules?'

'Ah! But it's not office hours any more, is it?'

'You're impossible!' Without giving him a

chance to stop her she walked out, but it was hard to retain her dignity with the mocking laughter that followed her.

That first day set the pattern of the others that followed. Ryan was teasing, annoying and faintly mocking, but never once did he treat her as a responsible employee in her own right. She began to have the feeling that to him this was only a game, that he never intended or wanted her in the office in the first place. He certainly didn't seem to accept her work as worth his serious attention either, and that she found hard to bear.

She had the strong feeling that he was just waiting for her to do something wrong before he asked her to leave, and it was only this that made her able to carry on with pretended indifference to his cracks. So she became careful and cautious, double-checking everything he asked her to do in case she missed some important point, all the time aware that he was waiting, like a cat at a mousehole, for her first mistake.

That first week she was so tired when she got home to her father's house that she had little energy to go out and see her friends in the evening, but by the Friday she felt that she had at last a good idea of how the company stood. It was as she had hoped. There was nothing very much wrong with Hall Bay; it was just in a temporarily vulnerable position because of the massive deal Ryan had set up in Singapore.

She was also forced to admit to herself that she

backed his ideas one hundred per cent. He had done the right thing, and it wasn't his fault that the money markets around the world had chosen to go haywire at a critical time for Hall Bay. She also knew why Brett Moncrieff was so busy trying to take them over. Ryan had walked off with the Singapore deal under Brett's nose, and he was not the kind of man to take that lying down. Indeed, the only thing that surprised her was the fact that he hadn't made her an outright offer for her shares in Hall Bay. That was something she found very peculiar indeed.

Feeling relaxed and lazy, she went up to her room to run a bath. She had cancelled most of her dates for this week, but tonight was going to be party night. There was a big charity ball and she had been asked to join a group of her friends for the evening. In fact she was quite looking forward to it because it would take her mind off herself.

Ryan's behaviour lay like an irritant at the back of her mind. Try as she might, she still found it impossible to banish him from her thoughts these evenings she was alone in the big house of her childhood. If only she knew what he really thought about her. That sensual awareness was still overpoweringly strong between them. He had maddened and irritated her this past week almost to the point of insanity, yet in spite of that her body was still far too aware of him, and she was fairly sure he felt exactly the same way. Why couldn't they trust each other?

She looked at her reflections in the triple mirrors on the dressing-table. Tonight she had left her hair loose, preferring for once the younger, softer image. Her skin looked glowing with health, her eyes enormous. The soft gold silk of her dress clung to the voluptuous curves of creamy gold flesh, broken only by a heavy gold necklace. The strapless dress showed off her two most remarkable assets so well that she grinned at herself in the mirror. She didn't think she would be exactly lacking in partners this evening.

Slowly she stood up and moved towards the long mirror hidden in the wardrobe. Yes, the dress was a success. Although it wasn't tight, the soft silk clung to her long legs as she moved lightly around her room. She felt good. Quickly she collected the short jacket, made of the same silk, and her evening bag, then, blowing herself a kiss in the mirror she ran lightly down the stairs.

William wasn't due to pick her up for another quarter of an hour, so, leaving her bag and jacket in the hall she slipped out into the garden, the warm air caressing her bare skin. It was nearly a full moon, low in the sky and glowing darkly orange. Two bands of cloud lay like broad stripes across its surface and just for a moment she frowned slightly as she gazed at the glowing luminous ball hanging so still in the velvet darkness of the night. Words flickered across her mind, but before she could pin down the elusive memory the sound of a car broke her train of thought, and she began to retrace her steps back up towards the house.

She knew who it was even before the dark shadow emerged into the light of the moon. 'You?' she whispered. 'I thought William was coming to collect me.'

'Would it have made that much difference? We're going in the same party after all.'

'Are we? I mean. . . I didn't know,' she finished painfully.

'Ah, Tara!' His voice was deep and caressing. 'Why do you always fight what's between us?' He moved closer to her. 'You are the most beautiful girl I've ever seen. I think you have bewitched me: those great eyes of yours, your wonderful, glowing skin. . . I dream of you next to me at nights, your wonderful, erotic body entwined with mine. . .' He gave a long sigh. 'I want you more than any woman I have ever met. I want to feel you in my arms, make love to you, breathe the very scent of you!'

Tara heard the passion in his voice and quivered in response. She wanted him! Oh, yes, she wanted him quite as much as he yearned to have her, but to what purpose? Her heart turned over painfully in her chest, thoughts fell about her in tumbling disorder. He doesn't love you, a cold hard voice told her, he doesn't even like you. . . He just wants your body. This is a trap. Remember seeing that rabbit caught in a snare? It hurt, didn't it? She drew a sharp breath in pain and denial, arguing with herself. No, this is different, she pleaded with herself. How different? the cold voice demanded. Remember the fortune-teller? 'When the moon wears the coat of the tiger, beware he who hunts in its light. . .'

Anguished, she turned away. 'Please, Ryan——' her voice cracked a little under the strain '—you know I can't do that. Why, you don't even trust me, so how can you think of taking me to bed?'

There was a tense silence.

'God knows!' He gave a jeering laugh. 'You're quite right too, because I don't trust you. I never have, right from the first moment I set eyes on you. But there's something about you that gives me no peace. You make me feel quite primitive. If I could get away with dragging you to some mountain cave then by God I'd do it and damn the consequences!'

There was another silence. A painful one for Tara, who fought hard to keep the tears from her eyes. His words had hurt, hurt so much, that the truth she had been keeping from herself jumped to the front of her mind. She had fallen in love with a man who neither liked or trusted her but who was prepared to go to almost any lengths to get her to sleep with him. A situation so fraught with danger that if she had any sense she'd pack her bags and leave on the first plane. Pain turned to outraged anger as she turned to face him.

'I wouldn't recommend you to try! The penalty for rape is a heavy one these days!'

He laughed. 'Oh, it wouldn't be rape, my dear! Once you were in my arms you'd consent quickly enough.'

'That's what you think!' she spat at him. 'I've called you arrogant before but I didn't realise the half of it. You may not be used to being turned down by my sex, but if you ever lay a finger on me again I'll go to Daddy and repeat what you've just told me.'

He infuriated her by laughing. 'Grow up, little girl! Don't you even understand yet that what's between us is a two-way thing? If you were truly indifferent to me, then this conversation would never have happened! OK, I accept that for the moment you want nothing to do with me. If a thing is worth waiting for—well, I've got all the patience in the world, as I hope you'll find out one day,' he continued outrageously, 'but I don't think Seb is going to get too hot under the collar over one kiss, do you? So, if you're going to worry him about it, why not wait until you've got something to really complain about?'

'And why don't you go and find someone else to give you relief from all that sexual frustration?' she yelled, driven almost beyond endurance.

'I'll do just that,' he grinned at her, 'just as long as you don't get the wrong idea if I do. Now let's forget the dramatics and go to the party. We've missed quite enough of it as it is.' He turned to walk up to the house, obviously expecting her to follow him.

She looked up at the moon, but as it had risen in the sky it had shed its orange glow. The clouds had moved, and now it shone gloriously down on her, the cold purity of its light quite without any pity or warmth.

CHAPTER SIX

GETTING into Ryan's car and going with him to the party was one of the most painful things Tara had ever had to do, but pride came to her rescue. Never, she vowed, would he guess that what had happened between them this evening caused her anything but anger. She took refuge in sarcasm, but Ryan seemed to be completely at ease, almost as if he had forgotten what had just taken place between them.

'Relax,' he told her, patting her knee as she strove to stop her body leaning towards his as he took a corner fast. 'You're quite safe. Think of me as your uncle.'

'Age-wise I suppose that could be true,' she replied waspishly, 'but your behaviour so far hasn't exactly encouraged me to see you in such a light.'

'Ah, but you don't know me very well yet, do you? I'm kind to animals and children—in fact my niceness is notorious throughout the whole colony.'

'That you're notorious I've already heard, but children and animals didn't come into it.'

He laughed. 'Miaow! The pussycat's got claws, has she?'

She risked a glance at his profile under the street lights and was annoyed to see that he was still grinning.

'In fact,' he continued conversationally, 'I don't know why I'm surprised. Those great tawny eyes of yours should have warned me. Cat's eyes, that's what they are, and when you're angry the pupils get large and black.'

Tara took refuge in silence, the pain at his laughter almost overwhelming her. In fact she was so caught up in the violence of her feelings that she refused to respond to any more of his teasing remarks, and when they arrived at the hotel she left him with pleasure while he went to park the car.

She should have been pleased when he devoted himself to a vivacious redhead who had newly arrived in Hong Kong, she told herself, but contrarily she was not. The other men in the party appeared young and shallow in comparison to him, and although she was treated with flattering attention by all of them it didn't make her feel better. Time began to drag, and she found it extremely difficult to keep her eyes away from Ryan and his chosen partner.

Rescue came in the unlikely shape of Brian Bourne, her father's racehorse trainer. He swept her away to dance, and she had every intention of trying to stick to him afterwards. In fact he made it easy for her.

'You look great, girl!' he told her, his eyes

inevitably fastening on her cleavage. 'In fact, if I were only ten years younger. . .'

'Shame on you! What if Scilla heard you?' Tara was referring to his extremely pretty second wife, who she'd met the other day.

'Scilla wouldn't mind! She'd take it as a compliment.'

'A pretty back-handed one,' she replied smartly, but Brian took her answer seriously.

'No, not really. It would show her that her husband has still got good taste!'

She laughed. 'I don't think I would be happy if I heard my husband say that to another woman, but as I'm not married yet maybe I could be wrong.'

'I'm sure it's not for lack of asking!' He continued in this slightly heavy-handed line of gallantry while he piloted her rather clumsily around the dance-floor. Tara was so grateful though for him taking her away from Ryan that she allowed him to flirt with her. 'By the way, there's someone on our table who's dying to meet you. He's just come over from the States. You interested?'

'Why not?' she parried lightly, trying to ignore Ryan's suddenly watchful eyes as he tried to dance his partner closer to her. I might have guessed he'd still have me under observation, she told herself bitterly, as she left the dance-floor with Brian. Then another thought entered her head with blinding suddenness. Why, he doesn't like or trust Brian either! A strange exultation made her cling on to Brian's arm as she half turned her head back to the dance-floor to give Ryan an enigmatic half-smile. It widened as she caught the beginnings of a frown before turning her attention back to her partner.

'What's he like, Brian?'

'Mike Hardwick? Well, he's good-looking enough to have held Scilla's attention all evening, but he's kind of fun too. I'm not sure how long he's out here for, or why, but he sure knows his racing!'

A man got up as they approached the table, and Tara was able to see just why Scilla looked a little put out at their arrival. About six feet tall, blond hair with more than a hint of red in it, and a boyish open face liberally spattered with freckles. The eyes were a vivid blue under brows and lashes several shades darker than the hair. A lazy smile just tilted the ends of a wide, generous mouth. It was a face of engaging, infectious charm and Tara responded unthinkingly with a smile as she reached forward to shake the hand held out to her.

'I'm very pleased to meet you, Miss Halliday.'

She noticed that the eyes had checked her figure, but not outrageously so, before returning to her face. 'Hello,' she responded warmly. He didn't seem to have much of an American accent, more of an English one. 'I gather you wanted to meet me?'

'I had the pleasure of meeting your father briefly when he was in LA. I'm sorry to hear that he's not been too well, but I gather it isn't anything serious?' He pulled up an empty chair as he spoke, and she sat down after smiling an acknowledgement to Scilla.

'We hope not. It's more in the nature of a warning to him to take things a little more easily in the future.'

'About time too!' Brian growled next to her. 'He's been working too damned hard these last few years. In the old days he'd never miss seeing one of his horses race, but latterly there have been several occasions when he's missed out. Which reminds me—why haven't you been out to the races since you've been back?'

'I didn't have anyone to take me.'

'That's no excuse. You know you'd only to lift the phone.'

'OK, OK!' She held up her hands. 'I plead guilty, but I've been busy this last week.'

'Why don't you come with us tomorrow?' Scilla asked. 'Your father's filly Merrymeet is running, isn't she, Brian?'

'Yes, and for the last time this season although I don't give her much chance of winning.'

'It would give me great pleasure if you'll come as my guest,' Mike Hardwick interrupted. 'I'll look after you better than these professionals.'

'Why, thank you, I'd enjoy that very much, but we can still all go together, can't we?'

Tara knew from Scilla's smile that she had said the right thing, and hoped she wasn't going to be treading too much on her toes by enjoying Mike's company.

'Come on, love! It's about time you danced with me.' Scilla gave in with good grace to her husband, leaving the two of them isolated at one end of the large table.

'Do you want to dance, Miss Halliday?'

'Call me Tara, please.' She smiled at him. 'If you don't mind I'd rather sit down for a bit.'

'I don't mind at all,' he smiled at her, 'and my name's Mike.'

'How long are you planning to stay in Hong Kong?' she asked.

'That's a bit of an open question at the moment. I work for a bloodstock agency, and we're looking into the idea of setting up a branch over here.'

'Great! So that's how you met Daddy, then?'

'Not quite. We met at the home of a mutual acquaintance, Slim Blackman. You know him?'

'No, I don't think so——' she wrinkled her brows '—although I think I've heard the name somewhere.'

'He's one of the biggest breeders in the States. He has a stud in Virginia and he bred this year's Derby winner.'

'That sounds like Daddy! Forgive me, but you don't have an American accent. Am I right?'

'Yes. I was born in Sydney, but I have an American mother so my time has been pretty evenly divided between the two countries.'

'But you don't sound Australian,' she protested.

'Well, I've been pretty much of a rolling stone these last few years, working a lot in Europe, so I suppose the accent's all rubbed off. Anyway I was educated in England.'

'That explains it!' she laughed. 'What is it about an English public school education that makes you all sound alike?'

'The desire to conform for a peaceful life, I expect. It'd take a stronger character than mine to stand out from the herd. Hey, am I breaking up anything important, by the way? There's a guy out there on the dance-floor who's been giving me black looks ever since you sat down.'

Tara didn't need to turn round to know who it was. Pain mixed with other emotions made it easy for her to answer. 'No. All the same, Mike, I'm supposed to be with another party so I'd better get back. I'm staying at my father's house—do you know where it is?' She stood up, and he joined her.

'Sure. I'll be along to collect you tomorrow. You'll have lunch with me?'

'Yes, I'll look forward to it. No, don't bother to come with me—I'll take this as an excuse to go and tidy myself.'

He smiled. 'You don't look as if you need it, but as I'll see you tomorrow I'm prepared to let you go now.'

She walked away with mixed feelings. Mike was easy to talk to and very attractive, and yet she felt there was something lacking in him, something not quite right. For all his open manner and face, she had the feeling that there was something guarded about him, very much at odds with the appearance he presented to the world.

Ryan was waiting for her when she came out of the ladies' cloakroom. 'Still spying on me?' she queried sarcastically.

'Keeping an eye on you,' he retorted, 'and by God you need it! Who was that character Bourne introduced you to?'

'That's none of your business!' she snapped. 'Anyway, what you have done with your partner?'

'Dished her. I couldn't concentrate on her while I had to keep an eye on you.'

'When will you get it into your thick head that I don't want you keeping an eye on me?' she shouted.

'Keep your voice down! Everyone will think we're quarrelling.'

'And what's wrong with that? It's true, isn't it? Will you please keep away from me?'

'No, and will you shut up for a minute? I heard from your father tonight. They're expected home on Sunday.'

'Sunday? Oh, that's great!' She was suddenly suspicious. 'When did you hear that?'

'I had a call just before I came to collect you. That's why I took William's place.' He watched with amusement as her bosom heaved with the mixture of emotions she was feeling.

'And why couldn't you have told me earlier?' she asked through gritted teeth.

'Don't tell me you've forgotten already what we were talking about?' he answered in a shocked voice. 'That was so important it put everything else out of my mind.'

'I don't find that amusing!'

'No, I can see you don't—your eyes are going black. . .'

'Ryan!'

He heard the menace beneath the single world, and shrugged his shoulders. 'I had to have some excuse to get you to talk to me, didn't I? By the way, I promised your father that I'd see you home. I hope you aren't going to make me break that promise?' She saw the laughter in the blue eyes as he watched her, and realised, belatedly, that he was enjoying seeing her over-react to his teasing.

Everything began to take on the quality of a nightmare. Whenever she was with Ryan he seemed to be able to wrong-foot her, put her in impossible situations. The light-hearted teasing became too much. She turned away in defeat, but not before he had the chance to catch the glimmer of tears in her eyes.

'Hey, sweetheart, what is it? I didn't mean to really upset you, you know that. . .' The genuine warmth in that deep voice almost broke her, but as he put an arm round her shoulders she stiffened.

'I'll just collect my jacket.' Without looking at

him she fled again to the one place where he would not be able to follow her. Once away from him it didn't take her long to remember all he had said to her earlier that evening. As she stood in front of the mirror and looked at the image reflected back she reminded herself yet again of her vow not to give herself to a man who did not love her.

In fact, when she rejoined him, after one searching glance at her face he behaved perfectly normally, and if there was more real warmth in his voice when he spoke to her than she was used to, she found it easy to put this aside as she concentrated only on listening to his amusing comments on the people who had been at the party, without having to say much herself.

She woke up the next morning feeling low and depressed after a restless night. Even the thought of her father returning couldn't banish the ache in her heart when she remembered Ryan and what he had told her yesterday evening.

Why had she fallen in love with him? To start with she had mistrusted him almost as much as he did her, so how could she have allowed herself to fall in love with such a man? OK, now she accepted that he seemed to have the interests of Hall Bay very much at heart, so perhaps she had misjudged him initially, but if she could see that, then why couldn't he accept the same about her?

The words of the Chinese fortune-teller came into her mind. 'When the moon wears the coat of

the tiger, beware of he who hunts in its light. He
will have the power to tear the heart from your
breast. . .' She lay back on the pillows remembering, remembering the strange orange glow of the
moon with the tracing of clouds across its face like
the stripes of a tiger. . . Fanciful, yes, but the truth
behind the words hit her forcibly. What was the
rest? Oh, yes! She was in danger, which would be
imposible to avoid unless she returned to the West
very soon.

Lethargically she got out of bed. Danger! Well,
she knew what that was all right; she was in
danger of breaking her heart over a man who
wanted her body, but cared nothing for her as a
person. She wished she had not agreed to go
racing today; she wanted time alone to come to
terms with her problem. The first thing she
accepted as she lay in the bath was that she could
no longer go on working at Hall Bay. That would
be too much; to see him every day, to know that
the strong sexual awareness between them would
tighten and strengthen whenever they were near
each other—no, that would be too much. . .

She was trying to force herself to eat something
for breakfast, rather than just coffee which she was
all she'd been able to face so far, when a letter was
delivered to her. Flora, the Filipino maid, told her
it had just arrived by courier. Slowly she opened it
to see that it was at last the long-awaited offer for
her shares in Hall Bay, but her brows rose with

surprise when she saw what she was being offered.

It was a huge sum, enough to give her independence for life if she accepted it. Her lips pursed in a soundless whistle. Brett Moncrieff had to be pretty desperate to go so high. Leaving it by her plate, she stood up in a determined manner. At least the offer had sparked her back into life, she thought wrily, as she walked through to her father's study. She sat down at his desk and, taking some writing-paper, formally refused the offer. She wasn't too surprised to notice that it was Marcel Chang's bank who were the acting agents.

'Flora?' she called, walking back into the big drawing-room. 'Can you ask Mr Chu to deliver this letter at once, please? Tell him it's important.'

'OK, Miss Tara. Mr Ryan's here waiting to see you. He's out on the terrace having some. . .'

But Tara hadn't waited for her to finish—she left the room in a rush. Her heart sank as she saw him studying the papers she had so stupidly left behind.

'I might have guessed that you'd be the sort of man to read other people's letters!' she said bitterly.

He looked up at her then, his eyes brilliantly blue in the sunlight. 'Good morning, Tara. If it was so important then why did you leave it lying around?'

'If I'd known you were going to arrive I'd have taken more care!' she snapped. She was aware that his cool intelligence was working overtime as he studied her face carefully; looking for clues, she thought scornfully. Well, he wasn't going to get any joy from her if she could help it.

'May I?' She held out her hand, and reluctantly he handed over the letter. Carefully she folded it, then put it away in her white bag.

'I suppose it's no use asking what you intend to do?' he asked quietly.

'No use at all, Ryan. You'll have to possess your soul in patience until Daddy returns tomorrow,' she purred.

'It's an exceedingly generous offer. Most people would be only too pleased to accept it.'

She heard the question in his voice. 'Would they?'

'Indeed they would. Hang it all, Tara! Can't you see that this is extremely important to me? I need to know what you intend to do about it!'

She was pleased to see that he had at last lost his cool. She raised her eyebrows in faint surprise. 'I thought you'd already decided what I would do?'

'Stop playing games with me.' His voice had gone quiet, and with a little *frisson* of fear she saw the eyes were now ice-cold. The fear made her feel aggressive. She knew she ought to tell him what she'd done, and if he hadn't behaved so badly last night she would have, she told herself. A feeling of recklessness filled her, and she gave a short laugh.

'I'm not playing games with you, Ryan, I never have. You're the one who likes games. It's a pity I don't know the rules, isn't it? If I did we might not be in this mess.'

'You little bitch! You're holding out on me because of what happened last night, aren't you? Do you think I don't know what's in your mind? You wanted to have me falling at your feet for the pleasure of kicking me away, didn't you? Well, you're never going to get me there! I've watched you very closely since you've arrived in Hong Kong. You've had most of the men you've met out here after you like bees round a honeypot, but you don't give a damn!

'You're a very sexy girl, Tamara Halliday, and don't you know it. But if you think I'm going to allow you to manipulate me, then think again. Those tricks might work on the young men you've met in your past but I'm too old to fall for that ploy. And another thing—I should watch out for that pretty young man Bourne introduced you to last night. He might look like God's gift to women, but I'm pretty sure his interest lies in quite a different area. I'm not sure why he should hang around you, and if you've got any sense you'll send him packing before you learn the hard way!'

He came and took her by the shoulders, ignoring the blazing fury in her face, and gave her a little shake. 'For God's sake, don't do anything about that offer until your father gets home, do you understand? Moncrieff's business empire isn't as solid as he'd like everyone to think. He needed that deal in Singapore that I took from him, and I think he's prepared to go to extraordinary lengths to get it back. When you corner a rat he gets nasty, Tara. If you're thinking of refusing that offer, don't do it in a hurry, that's all. OK?'

He let her go reluctantly, but the feel of his hands had already confused her emotions. Without consciously thinking, she asked the one question that had been worrying her.

'Why don't you like Brian Bourne?'

'I happen to know that he's in a financial mess. He's got no head for business and I think that second wife of his is expensive. . .' He stopped to look deep into her eyes. 'I also happen to know that he's mixed up with Moncrieff.' He saw the pain in her eyes. 'I'm sorry, Tara, but that's the truth.' He left her then, walking away quietly, leaving her alone with her thoughts.

By the time she came to her senses he had gone, and she was left feeling bereft and alone, which was crazy really when she thought how he'd just attacked her again. And yet, hadn't she detected an air of jealousy about the whole thing? With a little smile to herself she walked back to her father's study to complete the one thing she could think of that would help remove at least one barrier that was between them.

Ryan had only reinforced her own doubts about Mike Hardwick, so when he came to collect her she was pleasant but cool, not even inviting him into the house. She had the perfect excuse because she was outside talking to Mr Chu who had just returned. If Mike was slightly put out, he managed to hide it admirably. He took her in the taxi right through the heart of Wanchai down to Happy Valley itself, and they ate in one of the enormous Cantonese restaurants there, Tara making quite sure to keep the conversation non-committal on her part. Mike seemed quite happy to take his lead from her, so she began to relax a bit more in his company, even warning him that they'd better get a move on if they wanted to get in before the first race started.

She had forgotten what tremendous gamblers the Chinese were, as they fought their way through the enormous, jostling crowd towards the members' enclosure.

'My God—I'm glad racing isn't quite this popular in the States and in Europe!' He wiped his face with his handkerchief, the great mass of people around them combined with the humidity obviously too much for him.

'Better get used to it,' Tara reminded him unkindly, 'that is, if you're really set on opening up a bloodstock agency here?'

He heard the question in her voice, and gave her a disarming grin. 'My boss is!'

'Bad luck!' She grinned, suddenly grateful for his laid-back approach to her. Once in the enclosure she was fairly sure Scilla would soon find them, then she'd be able to slide gracefully into the background. She still hadn't managed to find out any particular reason why Mike should have been so keen to meet her, and had ended up concluding that he must see her as another contact with her father.

'There you are, darlings!' As Tara had hoped Scilla soon swallowed them both up, linking arms between them as she walked them towards the private boxes. 'Marcel's expecting you both! He's got two runners this afternoon, did you know?'

'Marcel?' Tara queried. 'Do you mean Marcel Chang?'

'Yes. He's just bought four more horses from Brian, so he's pretty special with us at the moment, my dear, as you can imagine.' Tara heard the purring satisfaction in Scilla's voice with a little misgiving. The Chinese, owners and punters alike, took their racing very seriously indeed. To win the right in the Jockey Club's annual ballot to buy, train and race a horse was the most fiercely sought and highly prized accolade of all, probably worth more than a mention in the Queen's Honours list. Mike with his bloodstock connections she could understand being invited; business was business, after all, but she couldn't understand why Marcel Chang should have invited her unless it was to do with her letter of refusal that she had sent this morning.

She hung back. 'I don't think I ought to go, Scilla. You two go on and leave me; I'll be fine here.'

'Nonsense!' Mike had moved swiftly around to her other side. 'Any man would want to have you in his box, even if it's just for decoration!'

Scilla laughed, but her grip tightened on Tara's arm. 'Don't be silly, Tara! I gather you had dinner together not so long ago. He's a charming man, I think—didn't you find him so?'

'Yes, I did, but really, Scilla, I'd rather not be included in his party this afternoon.' She stopped walking, determined not to go through the passage that led to the boxes. Both frowned at her, obviously disconcerted at her refusal to go any further. It was Scilla who took her to one side.

'Please, darling,' she whispered, 'do it for us. Brian and I have been having a bit of a hard time just lately. Marcel Chang has been our saviour, and he really wants to see you this afternoon. I promised you'd be there! Don't let us down, please?'

Tara couldn't help but feel the desperate sincerity behind the words. 'OK,' she replied slowly, 'but don't expect me to stay there long, will you?'

'No, no! If you'll just come, that'll be fine.'

Tara looked up to see Mike watching her with a hard, flat expression on his face, but as soon as he noticed her looking at him he gave one of his charming smiles. The change was so quick she wondered if she had been mistaken, as she and Scilla slowly rejoined him.

'Come on, you two! If we don't hurry you'll miss the first race.' He linked arms with the two of them, hurrying them along the wide passage, checking numbers, until he stopped. Opening the door, he stood back to usher her in, then followed her quickly, shutting the door behind him in Scilla's face. Standing facing her were Brett Moncrieff and Marcel Chang. She turned to leave, but Mike stood in front of the door, and he shook his head at her, his expression once more shuttered and cold.

CHAPTER SEVEN

Shock made sure that Tara said nothing. What indeed could she say? She knew perfectly well what those two men wanted of her, and she now bitterly regretted her impulsive refusal of Brett's offer this morning. Why hadn't she told Ryan what she'd done? Her pride and her disbelief in the lengths Brett would go to had landed her in this mess.

'Unless you're more stupid than I give you credit for, you know perfectly well what we want from you. You have been made an offer that is extremely generous for your holding in Hall Bay. We would like you to reconsider it.' Brett Moncrieff today had none of the jolly *bonhomie* about him that she remembered as so much part of his personality. This was a cold, hard stranger.

Tara drew herself up tall. She must not let these men intimidate her, or even let them see that she was afraid. She raised her eyebrows in pretended surprise. 'I thought I made it clear this morning that I was not interested in your offer? Anyway, isn't this meeting just a little melodramatic? If you'd asked me I'd have been quite happy to come down to the bank to tell you that I won't change my mind.'

'I think you will. Your father's not been well, has he? A minor heart attack? You wouldn't want him to be worried into another, perhaps more serious one, would you?'

This time there was no way she could disguise her shock. 'You can't do anything like that! Why, this is just a business deal——'

'Indeed it is,' Brett interrupted, 'but accidents have been known to happen even in the best-run homes. . .'

Shaken, she turned to Marcel Chang, who had been standing, quite silent and inscrutable, as he listened to the two of them. Speaking in Cantonese she asked, 'You cannot condone this, surely? Why? I thought you were a friend. . .'

'I see no problem, Miss Halliday. You have been made a very generous offer for some shares. Why should I not wish to condone it? I am very happy that you are in such an enviable position.'

'But my father——' she started to protest, but he interrupted her smoothly.

'Your father is thinking of retiring. We all know that, so where is the problem? You owe no particular loyalty to Veryan Bay, I think?'

She turned away, her brain churning with half-formed thoughts. What was she to do? Fear for her father's well-being stopped her telling them that this morning she had transferred all the shares back to his name. Mr Chu had been ready to leave with the signed transfer of the share certificates and her letter to her father's lawyer when Mike had arrived. If she signed the paper in front of them now, it would be worthless, but if she gave in too easily then maybe they would be suspicious.

'Come and sit down, Miss Halliday.' Courteous as ever, Marcel Chang escorted her to a chair in front of the box. 'The first race is about to start. We will continue this discussion when it is over.' All three men ignored her, raising their race-glasses to watch the horses at the start, as they came to stand behind her.

Unseeing and unhearing, Tara sat, a totally blank expression on her face as the race began. This couldn't be happening to her! The whole thing began to take on the quality of a nightmare. Here she sat, surrounded on all sides by simply thousands of people, yet she was trapped and unable to leave. What would happen to her when they found out what she had done? She shuddered slightly. Maybe she would be all right, because of course without the shares she would be of no real interest to them. Her father, too, should be safe— there would be no point in harming him after this. She was the weak link in the chain, one that it would be easy to put pressure on. She guessed, feeling half sickened, that it was from her mother that Brett Moncrieff had found out about her shares in the first place. She would have encouraged him to gamble on gaining control of Hall Bay, no doubt telling him that her daughter would be only too happy to sell out.

The race ended, but even the roar of the crowd,

as the favourite won, did not disturb her. It was the glass of champagne that was put in her hand that brought her to her senses. Automatically she said, 'Thank you,' although when she saw it was Mike who had given it to her she felt like throwing it in his face. Suddenly she was filled with anger. 'So, Brett Moncrieff is your boss, is he?' she said to him, then lifting the glass to her lips, turned to the Australian. 'If you want to reward him for bringing me to you like a good dog, why don't you let him go ahead and set up a bloodstock agency over here? He spent most of lunch telling me how fantastic Hong Kong is, and how much he'd love to live here!'

She saw Mike's face blench as Brett answered, 'I think that's a great idea!'

She stood up gracefully, pleased at having got her own back for at least some of the humiliation she'd had to put up with in the last few minutes. It hadn't taken her long over lunch to find out that Mike loathed the heat and humidity, let alone the seething masses of people, and couldn't wait to get back to the States.

Brett came to stand close to her. 'You've no doubt come to a decision, Tamara. I hope for everyone's sake it has turned out to be the right one.' Smoothly he handed her his pen, and withdrew a sheaf of papers from inside his jacket.

'You needn't bother with those,' she replied scornfully, opening her bag. 'I still have your offer with me.' Slowly, with no particular hurry, she

moved over to the table, which was heavily laden
with bottles and glasses as well as a tempting array
of snacks. She stood disdainfully on one side as
Brett in his eagerness cleared some space for her
to write, gesturing Mike to bring up a chair for her
to sit down.

Tara waited until she saw he had the chair in his
hands. She had deliberately manoeuvred herself
into the position where the table was now between
her and the others, and, moving faster than she
ever had in her life she was at the door pulling it
open, then running flat out down the empty
passage. She heard Brett shout, then an appalling
crash, as if the table had been knocked over. She
couldn't stop the sudden burst of hysterical giggles
that threatened to overwhelm her as she tried to
visualise the scene that she had so recklessly left
behind. Aware that it wouldn't take long for Mike
Hardwick to be on her trail, once back in the safety
of the members' enclosure she slowed her pace,
intent on taking refuge in the nearest ladies' room
until she could get word to Ryan of her
predicament.

She was therefore more than a little disconcerted
to find Scilla sitting in front of one of the mirrors.
'Tamara! Are you all right?' Scilla spoke in a
vibrant whisper, attracting more attention that
way than if she'd shouted the words out loud.
They got some curious looks, but Tara managed to
defuse the situation by answering brightly,

'I'm fine!' Then coming to sit on the stool next

to the other woman she continued quietly, 'No thanks to you, though.'

'My God, I——'

'Shush, keep your voice down!'

'Sorry. Tara—what happened?'

'They tried to get me to agree to sell my shares in Hall Bay to Brett Moncrieff!'

Scilla gave her a horrified look. 'Did you—er—I mean, have you signed?'

'No.' Tara looked at herself in the mirror. She'd lost her hat in her mad dash, and looking at her hand she saw in amazement that she still had Brett's pen tightly clasped in it. Apart from that she didn't look too bad. Slightly pinker in the cheeks than normal, her hair untidy, with wide eyes still rather blank in expression, the aftermath of shock. 'Here, you'd better take charge of that. It doesn't belong to me,' she said quickly, handing over the pen.

'I don't want it! Who does it belong to, anyway?'

'Moncrieff, of course, who else?' Tara stared at Scilla, her face suddenly hard. 'Did you know they were going to try to force me into signing those papers?'

'No—no! I didn't know anything! Please believe me, Tara. I was horrified when Mike just shut the door in my face. I didn't know what to do!' Her face had gone quite white, and Tara was sure she was telling the truth.

'OK, I believe you. Now. . .' Tara gave her a

long, considering stare. 'How are you going to help me get out of here?'

'Help you? Oh, lord, they're not still after you?' Her hands had flown to her face, her voice had risen.

'Shush!' Tara frowned her down. 'I'll give you any odds you like that rat Mike Hardwick's waiting right outside the door. I bet he goes on waiting until racing's finished for the day as well.'

Scilla's pretty, rather vacuous face went quite blank. 'What are we to do?' she whispered. 'He won't let me go if he knows you're in here!'

'No, we've got to get help. Ryan will come fast enough if he gets to hear about it, but I don't know where he is.'

'He normally goes sailing on weekends,' Scilla replied, unhelpfully.

'Let me think.' Tara looked unseeingly into the mirror, her brain working frantically. Suddenly the gleam of an idea came into her head. 'Wait here!' she told Scilla, as she got up to talk to one of the Chinese attendants who was collecting used towels. What she learned put a sparkle back into her eyes.

'I think it's going to be all right. There's a back way out of here. . . Now, look—can you go outside and tell Mike that you saw me dash in here and lock myself in? That should make him happy, particularly if you start to give him hell for shutting that door in your face! You must make sure that he still believes me to be in here, otherwise they'll catch me outside. Please, Scilla? If you do that, I won't tell anyone about your part in all this.'

Scilla looked happy for a moment, then a frown came to her face. 'But what will happen to me when they find out that you've gone? They'll think then that I lied!'

Privately thinking that this was one of the least of her worries, Tara reassured her. 'Don't be stupid! I left while you were outside talking to Mike. If he starts to insist that you come back in, just give him hell for being so rude earlier. The longer you can spin that out, the more they'll believe you later.'

Scilla's eyes narrowed. 'That bastard! Don't worry, Tara, I'll do it. I wish to God that we'd never got mixed up in this mess, but Brian. . .' She broke off, obviously horrified at what she'd nearly let out.

'Just do what I say, and I'll forget it ever happened as far as you're concerned. Anyway, if it's going to work you'll have to go out soon, otherwise they might get suspicious that you're covering for me. Good luck!' They both stood up, Tara giving her a quick peck on the cheek. 'Don't let me down, Scilla. They managed to scare me, you know, in the box.' Their eyes met, Scilla's now a little frightened.

'What are you going to do?'

'It's better if I don't tell you, but don't worry, I'll be safe, as long as they believe I'm still in here!'

She gave the other woman a little push towards the door, retreating out of sight.

Later, in the taxi on the way to her father's house, she thought that never had money been better spent than in lavishly tipping the two cloak-room attendants who had made sure she got away safely. That didn't solve the problem of what she was to do next. Her first priority had to be letting Ryan know what had happened to her, and the veiled threats to her father.

When she called his apartment she was surprised he answered so quickly.

'Ryan?' she queried, hardly believing her luck at finding him at home on a Saturday afternoon.

'Tamara! Where are you?' She thought his voice sounded a bit harsh and was surprised.

'I'm at Daddy's——' She wasn't allowed to finish.

'Stay right there! I'm on my way.' The phone went dead. She shrugged her shoulders as she looked at it in astonishment before gently replacing it. At least it was good to know that he'd take care of any problems. One thing she was fairly sure about was that he was more than capable of taking care of her father and herself if Brett Moncrieff and Marcel Chang should try any further tricks.

She was beginning to feel exhausted after what had happened to her; it would be pleasant to drop her burdens on to shoulders more capable of carrying them.

She didn't have too long to wait before the
sound of a car driven fast had her heart beating a
little faster. She gave a smile of relief as she heard
the forceful footsteps crossing the marble floor of
the hall.

She tried to appear relaxed and casual, but the
feelings of excitement, mixed with shyness, had
her standing to greet him in a gauche manner quite
foreign to her normal behaviour as the double
doors burst open.

Tara got her second great shock of the day as
she saw his expression. He looked murderous,
and involountarily she took a step back as he
advanced purposefully towards her.

'You double-dyed scheming little bitch!' He
stopped a couple of feet from her, his eyes narrowed to two gleaming slits as he studied her face.
'Oh, you may well look surprised! You didn't think
this would be found out until Monday, did you?
By then of course you'd have been ready to leave,
having had your revenge. You had me fooled! The
stage should be your career, not business studies.
I should have trusted my instincts about you right
from the start, but you've been putting up a pretty
convincing act this last week. I really thought I had
misjudged you!'

Tara began to feel faint under the furious batter-
ing of his words.

'Yes, you might well look shattered! But there's
no honour among thieves. Moncrieff took great
pleasure in informing me you had signed over

your shares to him. You should have waited just that big longer, shouldn't you?' he taunted her cruelly.

'B-but—when——' The shock seemed to have affected her speech, but he was too impatient to wait for her to finish.

'He left a message for me early this afternoon. You should have taken that into account before you signed, Tamara, if you wanted to keep your part of it secret. He couldn't resist letting me know that he'd won after all.'

'No! You're wrong, wait——' she pleaded, tears in her eyes.

'Don't think you can soften me by your play-acting! I've got no interest in hearing you trying to justify your greed. You could well have your father's death on your hands after this performance. He knows what you've done, and wants you out of this house before he returns.'

'No!' She gave a small moan of real agony.

'Yes! I don't know what scheme you concocted with your mother to finally humiliate him, but Serena and I are agreed that he shall be spared that last indignity. You leave Hong Kong tonight!'

He threw a ticket down on to the table near her. 'That's your seat back to London, economy class. You leave this evening. Flora has packed all your things, and Chu is waiting to take you to the airport. It won't do you any harm to sit and wait there until your flight is called, but by God, if you try to stay and meet your father tomorrow, then

I'll personally see that you regret it for the rest of your life!' He turned on his heel and began to walk away, ignoring her pleas.

'Wait, Ryan! You're making a terrible mistake! Please wait!' He totally ignored her as she followed him out to the hall, where she was brought up short by the sight of her cases neatly standing in a row. By the time she had recovered herself sufficiently to follow him outside, the car was already in gear, the powerful engine whining into high revs as it roared away down the sloping drive. Shattered, she sank down on the front steps and burst into tears.

It was Flora, the Filipino maid, and Mr Chu who stopped her tears. 'It's all right, Miss Tara!' Chu held her arm, and Flora was patting her gently. She made a great effort to stop crying, and as Flora handed her a box of tissues blew her nose determinedly. 'It will be OK,' Mr Chu told her again. 'Listen, missy!'

She gave a rather watery smile at the name he had always called her when she was a small child.

'I know Mr Ryan wrong about you. When he tell me to book ticket for you, I do that and book another one same time.' He grinned at her shattered face. 'You go package holiday to Phuket for one week! OK? Flight leave in two hours!' He gave her a folder.

'Miss Tara—I pack special case for you. All ready for holiday. Chu will keep your cases in his flat here until you come home.' Flora beamed at her. 'Mr Ryan will be very, very sorry when he finds out the truth.'

Tara was so shattered by what had happened that she didn't know what to do. The only thing that was clear was that she had to leave. It didn't really matter where she went as long as she left Hong Kong. She tried to summon up a smile for the two conspirators, who watched her face eagerly for some sign of agreement.

She smiled and shrugged her shoulders in resignation. 'Thank you! I didn't want to go back to London so soon. My father. . .' She gave a big sigh.

'I tell him! I tell him tomorrow what I have done for you when I get him from airport. I tell him everything.' Mr Chu stood up proudly. 'He will be very sorry!'

'Now you must come and change quick for travelling.' Flora chivvied her into the house. 'There is little time!' Then she gave her a big smile. 'You will like Phuket. Very beautiful island, everyone say so. Easy flight from Hong Kong—no stops!'

Between the two of them Tara was given little time to stop and think. She warned Mr Chu to tell her father about the threats Brett Moncrieff had made to her that afternoon. The little man was horrified when he heard all that had happened to her at the racetrack, but when they were at the airport he smiled at her. 'You back very soon, I think. Have a nice holiday!'

Phuket was a beautiful island, surrounded by coral beaches, just off the southern end of Thailand in the Andaman Sea. It had been opened up for tourism, but so far not excessively so. The hotel where Tara was staying was newly built and modern, but as it was dark when she arrived she would have to wait until the morning to find out more. She had spent most of the flight asleep, so had been awake for much of the hour-long drive from the airport to the hotel.

The coach was full of couples, some English, some French, and what looked like Hong Kong businessmen with their Chinese mistresses. She was the only person who appeared to be travelling alone. Her heart filled with bitter sadness as she thought of what might have been. Fate seemed to be determined to separate her from her father. It felt alien and wrong to come on holiday by herself, but she accepted that Mr Chu had done the best he could in the circumstances. In fact, he had told her she was lucky, because it was high season and he had managed to get a last-minute cancellation.

She realised very quickly the next day that time was going to hang heavily on her hands unless she kept herself busy. The hotel was rather as she had feared; large and a little soulless, as so much resort architecture now seemed to be worldwide. The Thai people were charming, though, so friendly, and the island was paradise.

Soft silver sands, impossibly blue sea, with palms and casuarinas growing right down to the edge of the beach. She discovered that the hotel was really bed and breakfast, but there were so many little palm-thatched restaurants around the beach that there was no problem in eating delicious fresh food very cheaply.

She planned her days carefully. Early in the morning, learning to windsurf before it became too hot and while the wind was gentle. Exploring the sea with a mask and flippers became an enchantment, the small fish with their vibrant colours never seen before except in aquariums. Then lunch alone in one of the many small restaurants. The heat of the early afternoon was spent with a book in the shade of the hotel gardens, full of flame trees and purple bougainvillaea, among the lush green tropical vegetation, but it was unusual for her to turn many pages—her mind was too full.

She thought of Ryan with an aching longing day and night, wondering now that he knew the truth whether he would do anything about it, but as the days slowly passed by with no word she tried to force herself to accept that to him she was just one more girl, albeit one who had got away.

She was in the garden with her book on the afternoon of the fourth day when she became aware that someone else had arrived at what she now thought of as her private place. Studiously she ignored them, a slight frown deepening her brow. Plenty of men had approached her, either obliquely or directly, these last few days, but to all of them she had made it clear that she was just not interested in having her solitude disturbed.

She was aware that she was being studied comprehensively but she resolutely refused to have her attention diverted from her book. An unwilling laugh made her look up to see a tall man with grey hair and lively hazel eyes standing at the foot of her lounger.

'Well, well! That's quite a performance! Worthy of Garbo, I'd say. "Leave me, I want to be alone!"' he mimicked.

Shocked recognition had held her rigid, but the words unlocked her unnatural pose. The book went flying as she leapt up to run to him. 'Daddy!'

He held out his arms, and she let them close around her as she clung convulsively to the first man she'd ever truly loved. It seemed words weren't needed. Tara felt his love, as strong as her own, as she clung even tighter. It wasn't until this minute that she realised just what had been missing from her life all those long years. Her father's love had always been a haven in an uncertain world, and when she had been separated from him it hadn't taken long for the seeds of insecurity to grow deeply.

There were tears in her eyes as she loosened her grip to stand back and look at him. 'Are you all right? Really all right?'

'I'm "very fine", as you used to tell me when you were a child!'

'But what are you doing here? Is Serena with you?'

'No, darling. I've come alone to fetch my daughter back home where she belongs. But first I thought I'd join you for the rest of your holiday so we can get to know each other again with no distractions.'

'Oh, Daddy. . .' It was impossible now to hold the tears back and they poured down her cheeks as she faced him silently. He said nothing, just gave her his hankie and held her close to him, until she managed to regain control of her emotions.

Later, when they were both sitting on her lounger, she turned to him and said, 'I wish, oh, how I wish you hadn't been away when I arrived.'

'Yes, that has proved to be exceedingly unfortunate, but, to use a cliché, all's well that ends well, wouldn't you say?'

In the face of such quizzical humour there was little she could do but agree with him. If only she had heard from Ryan then her agreement would have been whole-hearted. Quite unable to help herself, she gave a little sigh. Her father hadn't even mentioned his name. . . Overcome with guilt for even thinking of him when she had just been reunited with her father made her give him a hug.

'Have you managed to get a room near mine?'

'No, not that near, I'm afraid. At one stage it looked as if you and I would have had to share! It was a shame Chu couldn't manage to get you into a slightly better hotel.'

'I think he did brilliantly to even think of sending me here,' she stoutly defended him, 'otherwise I could have been back in London by now.'

'True,' her father smiled at her, 'and don't worry. He's been suitably rewarded for his part in all this, I promise you.' He gave her a smile. 'Judging by your reactions when I first found you here, I think it's a good thing I've arrived. Have you had much trouble with the other guests?'

Tara shrugged. 'Not really; I can handle most things.'

'So I saw,' her father laughed, 'but I'm pleased that now I've arrived you won't be in such an awkward situation.'

'They'll probably think I'm your mistress!' She grinned back at him.

'Nonsense! Anyway, if they do we can soon disabuse them of any ideas like that. Now come on back with me to the hotel. I haven't had time to unpack yet, and I'm hardly suitably dressed to be on holiday, so I want to change.'

'I'll unpack for you,' Tara said eagerly, as they linked arms to walk slowly back.

'I hoped you would offer.' Her father grinned down at her in return. 'I've been spoilt since I married Serena—she looks after me almost too well.' He patted his stomach a little complacently.

'So I see!' his daughter responded. 'You probably don't get enough exercise just sitting around in your office all day.'

'Ah! But I hope that's going to change in the future. Let's order some tea, shall we? I could do with something to drink.'

'Tea?' Tara teased. 'Here you are on a tropical island with the most delicious fresh fruit drinks and you want tea?'

He laughed. 'I'm too old to change the habits of a lifetime now. Tea it is!' They took the lift up to his room, talking easily and companionably together. Nobody seeing them together would guess that they had not seen each other for twelve long years, Tara thought happily as she followed him into his room.

CHAPTER EIGHT

IT SEEMED to Tara quite a deliberate choice on both their parts that neither she nor her father talked about the present. Indeed they both had so much to catch up on that it wasn't until after dinner that her father at last asked her what had happened at the races last Saturday.

She told him bluntly, her voice a little flat. 'Brett and Marcel Chang thought they could intimidate me into signing away my shares. They implied you could be made to have another heart attack or an accident. . . I didn't want to give in too easily in case they became suspicious, but in fact I managed to get away. Scilla Bourne helped me.'

'Scilla helped you to get away?' She heard the disbelief in his voice.

'Yes, she did. In fact, if it weren't for her I'm not sure I'd have made it back to the house.'

'But I understood that it was she and Hardwick who handed you over, so to speak.'

'She didn't know what she was doing, Daddy. She was absolutely horrified when Mike shut the door in her face, and we both owe her a big thank-you.'

'I see. . .' Her father frowned, then took her hand. 'We should have trusted you all along the line. Can you forgive me for my part in this?'

Tara tried to blink away her tears. 'Don't be silly! Anyway, if it weren't for Ryan you'd never have known, would you?'

'Don't put all the blame on him, my dear. I'm afraid it was my decision to have you followed. He was acting on my instructions. . .'

'Oh!' Tara looked away out to the dark sea. The tiny lights of the fishing boats bobbed and glittered like small stars. She gave a great sigh, before turning back to her father. He looked worried, but the clasp of his hand on hers was still firm. 'I suppose I know who both of us must blame,' she answered quietly. 'If Mummy hadn't told Brett of my holding, then I don't suppose any of this would have happened. He took a gamble, no doubt encouraged by her to think I'd sell my shares.

Her father shook his head sadly. 'I didn't want to have to tell you, but I should have guessed that you'd have worked it out for yourself. I must have hurt her very badly that she should still, after all these years, want to hurt me back.'

'Yes, I think perhaps you did. She has never got over Serena, and I don't think she ever will.'

'Yet we weren't happy together, you know! I think our marriage was a mistake almost from the start. She always wanted more than I could give her. . .' He broke off, obviously unwilling to say any more.

'She'll be all right now,' Tara said in a positive tone. 'I think it was a pity she didn't leave me behind with you, because I must always have reminded her of her life in Hong Kong, and her unhappiness. Now I've gone, I think she'll be able to get on with her life instead of endlessly looking back into the past. She must have seen the break-up of your marriage as a failure on her part, and we both know that she hates to lose. She always tries to be the best.'

'I agree, she was always a remarkable woman in many respects. Is she happy with John Chacewater?'

'Oh, yes, I think so. She's a very good wife to him as well. He comes first with her all the time, so that's why I found it extraordinary that she should care so much about trying to get revenge on you.'

'You know the saying, a woman scorned and all that. . . There's always been a great deal of truth behind that particular cliché! Certainly for a woman of your mother's temperament.'

'I suppose so. . .'

'Don't look so sad, darling. Serena and I will try to make up to you for what you've lost. By the way, your shares are back in your name again.'

'Oh, no, Daddy! Brett might try again!'

'No way! He's burnt his fingers badly trying to take us over, but he's too good a businessman to waste time on a lost cause. We're now in a strong enough position to fight back, and he knows that. What he tried to do to you was disgraceful, but you needn't worry about him. He won't show his face in Hong Kong for a very long time to come.'

'What about Marcel Chang?'

'Ah! The Jockey Club weren't at all pleased to hear about the way you'd been treated. I would be surprised if he wins a right in the next ballot. Or if he does, it will have cost him a very great deal of money.'

'And Brian Bourne?'

'He's been a bloody fool!' her father exploded. 'I told him that after this I was seriously considering removing all my horses from his stables.'

'Don't write him off on my account, please,' Tara pleaded. 'You've been together for so many years, and if it weren't for Scilla's help. . .' There was a short silence.

'I suppose that does make a difference. Although it beats me why you want to save that old reprobate. My God! When I think what could have happened if you had signed that form. . . It hardly bears thinking about.'

Tara strove for a little light relief. 'You have been busy on my behalf. I thought you were supposed to be taking things easily for a bit?'

'Don't worry—Ryan has taken care of most of it.' Her father now gave her a searching look. 'He's decided, by the way, that the two of you can't work together. Is that true?'

Tara felt her heart twist with anguish. So, she had been right all the time, but at least she could try to save her pride. 'Yes,' she replied slowly, 'I would agree.'

'But why?' She was surprised at the concern she heard in his voice, and looked up at him, startled. 'It has been my dearest wish that the two of you might get together. From what Serena told me, I thought it was more than possible it was on the cards.' He looked at the deliberately blank expression of her face carefully. 'Is it because of what he said to you on Saturday?'

She had no need to disguise the truth. 'No, it's not that. Look, Daddy, he's just not the kind of man that I. . .' She broke off. 'Let's just leave it, shall we?' This was awful. Her father's words hurt as much as if he had struck a knife into her very being. How could she tell him that it was her dearest wish as well? He might, horror of horrors, even give Ryan a hint, and Ryan might feel obliged to act on it, particularly after what he had said to her on Saturday.

'Far be it from me to push you into a marriage you don't want, but I must say I don't understand what's gone wrong between the two of you. Ryan's had most of the women in Hong Kong after him for years, yet you seem to be impervious to all that charm.'

At all costs her father must not learn how she felt. She wouldn't be able to bear it if Ryan was—well, kind to her for all the wrong reasons. She tried to summon up some of that old anger.

'Perhaps that's why!' she answered scornfully.

'Anyway,' she continued, 'I can't imagine why you thought there was anything going on between us in the first place!' She couldn't resist trying to find out if there was just a little hope.

'Serena seemed to think. . .'

Hope vanished, squashed in a haze of illogical pain. 'Serena was wrong!' This time her father couldn't deny the obvious sincerity in her voice.

'OK, OK!' He put up his hands in mock surrender. 'But if you'd ever heard Ryan describing you, then maybe you might change your mind.'

A little wave of hope rose again before being instantly dashed by that uncomfortable inner voice of hers.

'There's a great deal of difference between love and lust,' she told him severely, trying to hold her feelings in check, but it seemed he realised that he might have gone too far.

'All right, darling, I get the message. But I've got one for you in exchange. He wants to see you on your return to Hong Kong, I think to apologise.'

'You can tell him from me that he's got no need to apologise. I understand why he lost his temper, and that's the end of it as far as I'm concerned.' Sheer panic at the thought of seeing him again forced that out of her.

Her father shrugged his shoulders as he stirred his coffee. 'OK, if that's what you want.' Tara was too caught up in her own thoughts to catch his quick amused glance at her face. She's fighting something, he told himself with pleasure as he tried to think up some topic of conversation that would not be quite so controversial. 'By the way, I'm giving a large party to welcome you back to Hong Kong.' This tactic proved as successful as he hoped it would.

'A party? For me?'

'A party, just for you! Let me have a guest-list before we get home, will you? I gather you've got quite a lot of friends out here just now, but we'll include old friends as well, shall we?' He smiled with pleasure as he saw that she seemed ready to put her problems to one side. 'Serena's already started planning it, but no doubt she could do with some help when we get home. Anyway, it'll help to keep you out of mischief until we find something for you to do.'

A shadow crossed her face as he said that, but he ignored it, successfully diverting her thoughts to other channels.

Two weeks later she was up in her room getting ready for the party. She had neither seen nor heard from Ryan since that fatal Saturday and illogically she was furious that he hadn't tried to get in touch with her. She told herself he owed her something for having treated her so badly, but there hadn't even been a bunch of flowers to assuage her hurt.

She knew also that he would be at the party tonight; not that anybody had said anything, but she guessed that he would have had an invitation.

Both Serena and her father had been the soul of tact, so much so that perversely it had annoyed her. His name had not been mentioned in front of her, and because of what she'd said to her father it was quite impossible for her to talk about him.

This morning a parcel had been delivered to her, and when she'd opened it she'd been amazed to see the beautiful piece of jade that Brett Moncrieff had given her. It had been accompanied by a short note.

'The word is out that Ryan has at last bowed to pressure and is to give up his bachelor status in exchange for the controlling interest in Hall Bay. I promised you this as a wedding present, but it's come a little sooner that I expected. I admire your guts, Tamara, but think you are worth better than being used as a pawn in a business merger. You would have been better off accepting my offer! Brett.'

Much as she wanted to dismiss the note as poisonous nonsense she wasn't able to because of what her father had said to her. Hurt pride mixed with pain until she consoled herself with remembering that nothing had happened. If a small voice whispered 'yet' to her, then she was able to squash it. The day had been so busy that she had managed to push the words into the back of her mind, but now she was alone in her room they possessed her to the exclusion of all else.

Her new dress was a wonderful acid-green silk that made her hair look distinctly tawny and

showed up her tan. Her father had given her a
beautiful choker of pearls for her twenty-first birthday present, the central clasp made of emeralds
and diamonds. The dress was strapless, with a
tight bodice and a mini-skirt showing off her long
legs, and she knew Serena didn't really approve of
it, thinking it made her look too sexy, but she
thought it was great.

At least she had been happy with it until this
morning. The thought that Ryan, too, might find
her irresistible in it, even to the point of proposing
marriage, had her feeling faint. She sat down
hurriedly in front of the mirror.

She was struck by the incongruity of the prayer
she was saying silently under her breath. 'Please,
Lord, don't let Ryan ask me to marry him this
evening.' Before Brett's letter, she had just as
easily begged the Lord to make him fall in love
with her. Her lip trembled; waves of hopeless love
and longing swept over her as she faced the truth.
If Ryan should indeed propose, then she would
accept on the principle that half a loaf was better
than none.

These two weeks with no sight of him had
proved conclusively that she was head over heels
in love. When it came down to the basics, hurt
pride just didn't come into it. How many times
had she been tempted to wait outside his apartment for a sight of him? She'd even gone to the
lengths of making up excuses to visit her father at
Hall Bay, until fear that he'd see through her had

stopped her. All the petty humiliations that came
with being in love with someone you weren't sure
returned it had been her lot these last weeks.

She knew that Serena had been surprised at her
restless, unsettled state of mind. Tara had told her
it was because she hadn't got a proper job any
more, but she wasn't sure that Serena believed
her. If only there'd been someone she could talk
to about him, but her best friend was back in
London, and she didn't trust any of the girls out
here. So many of them were a little in love with
him themselves.

A soft tap at the door disturbed her.

Flora slipped in. 'Oh, my!' she giggled. 'You
look real good in that dress, Miss Tara!'

'You think so?' She stood up and gave a twirl.
'You don't think it's too short?'

'Oh, no!' She got an admiring look. 'You're
going to have all the men after you this evening.
Mr Halliday, he wants you downstairs, Miss Tara.
He says to tell you that people will be arriving any
minute now!'

'OK, tell him I'll be down in a minute.'

Tara had known that it was inevitable that she and
Ryan would have to dance together. She had
managed very well to keep out of his way most of
the evening, not being exactly short of partners,
but like two magnets they were drawn closer and
closer to each other as the evening progressed. It
was impossible for her to pretend to herself that

she was unaware of him, and she knew that he knew it.

Ryan played the waiting game so skilfully that when the inevitable happened she went with him without a murmur of protest. She allowed him to dance her outside on the terrace, and then to lead her down into the black shadows of the garden which had been dimly lit with lanterns.

He held her in his arms with a sort of hungry tenderness before his mouth found hers in a kiss of such passionate longing that she melted with delight. Time ceased to have any meaning as they clung to each other with a vibrant sensuality. He, by pressing his body so close to hers that she was almost painfully aware of his acute arousal, inflamed her own desires to an almost uncontrollable pitch.

A loud splash, followed by laughter and cheers, had both of them moving apart from each other. Tara was filled with such a complicated mixture of emotions that she hardly knew whether to laugh or cry, but one thing was certain: she was unable to speak. She risked one quick look at his face and what she saw there made her catch her breath. It was the sight of a strong man so caught up in his desire that he seemed curiously helpless. The flared nostrils above lips clamped closely together, the glittering eyes, half shut by heavy lids, and overall the impression of hopeless acceptance that he was caught up in feelings so strong that he was having to use all his will to hold them in check.

'Oh, dear God!' she whispered, shattered to see such a display of naked agony, yet unable to move.

'Tara! Tara, where are you?' The laughing voice of one of her friends broke the spell, and she turned quickly to run lightly up the steps, back towards the safety of the noise and laughter of the finishing stages of a successful party. Ryan mustn't be found with her looking like that; he deserved the privacy of being left alone in the dark garden to pull himself together before he left. Now was not their moment, even if she did feel as dizzy and exhilarated as if she had drunk to much champagne. He would not risk seeing her again this evening, of that she was sure, but it was impossible to stop her heart beating its own wild tattoo.

Tara had been convinced that she would not sleep when she eventually got to bed, but intense emotions took their toll of the body. She crashed out almost as soon as her head touched the pillow, not waking until Flora came into her room with breakfast very late the following morning.

It was obvious she was lingering because she wanted to talk, but Tara had noticed an envelope on the tray with her name written in a distinctive, spiky hand. She pretended to be sleepy so Flora reluctantly left her. Once alone she sat up briskly, but her fingers were trembling as she clumsily tried to slit the envelope.

The note was short. 'Can you meet me at my apartment for lunch today? We have to talk.' It was signed quite simply with his name. Lunch today! In a sudden panic she noticed the time. She threw off the bedclothes and leapt out of bed, breakfast forgotten, except to pour herself a reviving cup of black coffee.

After her bath she tried on then discarded so many of her clothes that her room began to look like the changing-room of a dress shop. She ended up in a square-necked dress of a simple white lawn so fine that she had to wear a camisole top beneath it. The skirt was lined and gathered lightly at the waist, and she added a raspberry-pink wide suede belt, and pink shoes. Naturally her hair had chosen to be rather wild and unmanageable that morning, so she tied it back with a white ribbon.

'Flora?' she yelled, running down the stairs.

'Yes, Miss Tara?' She appeared rather quickly from the kitchen, obviously hoping that Tara was now going to discuss the party exhaustively with her.

'I've got to go out. Have you seen my father anywhere?'

'They've both gone for lunch at Government House.'

'Oh, of course! I'd forgotten. Can you tell them I'm not sure when I'll be back, but not to worry?'

'OK. You going to see Mr Ryan?'

'What? Oh, yes, then I'm going on somewhere else.' Tara tried to be natural and casual, but it was difficult in the face of Flora's knowing grin. 'I've left my room in a terrible mess. Don't worry about it, I'll tidy it myself when I get back.'

'OK. You want a taxi?'

'I've already rung for one! Bye. . .' Without waiting any longer she ran out of the house into the drive, tapping her foot impatiently as she waited for the taxi to come and collect her.

The sun was already hot, and she could feel small beads of perspiration on her face. She took out a tissue, telling herself to calm down. It would have been more sensible to have waited in the cool of the air-conditioning, but she was too much on edge to have faced any more of Flora's questions.

When the taxi eventually arrived she was in a fever of impatience. Would she and Ryan be alone? The butterflies leapt in her stomach. Oh, no! Now her tummy was going to rumble—she should have eaten something for breakfast.

It was Ah Chee who let her into Ryan's apartment, and at the sight of the smiling Chinese face her heart sank. This was to be no romantic lunch à deux after all. She was intrigued to notice that the apartment couldn't have been more different from his office. Luxurious, filled with antiques and large soft sofas, the kind that really enticed you to lie back and relax against the cushions. Alarmed at the path her thoughts were taking her, she moved over to admire an enormous orchid plant that was heavily in flower. A door opened and shut quickly, then Ryan was with her.

She was amazed to see that he was formally dressed in an extremely smart dark suit, yet he looked a little haggard as if he had not enjoyed a particularly good night's sleep.

'It was very good of you to come, Tara. I hope you're not too tired?'

Disconcerted at his polite but distant manner, she answered him somewhat at random. 'No, I'm fine. . . I've just been admiring all this. . .' She moved one arm rather too generously and knocked a small Fo dog on to the thick rug. 'Oh, no!' She quickly picked it up, concern in her face as she turned it around in her hands. 'It's all right, I think,' she qualified nervously, as she replaced it.

'Of course it is.' He gave her a quick smile. 'Now, what I can get you to drink?' He moved over to a tray which had an unopened bottle of champagne and a jug of orange juice with two glasses.

'That looks fine to me.'

'With or without orange?' her queried.

By now Tara was beginning to feel in need of whatever support she could get. 'Without.'

The champagne was opened expertly with a satisfying plop. He poured out two glasses, handing one to her.

'Cheers!' He raised his glass to her, and she followed suit but took too big a gulp, so ended up with a choking fit. He ignored it, and, feeling stranger by the minute, she came to sit rather primly next to him on one of the big sofas. 'It was a good party last night. I hope you enjoyed it?'

'Very much, thank you.' They weren't going to

make polite small talk forever, were they? she asked herself. But it seemed he hadn't finished yet.

'I think your father looks remarkably well considering everything, don't you?'

She took a deep breath, trying to ignore the powerful body sitting so close to hers. 'Very well. I think now he's decided to retire he's become more relaxed.'

'Yes. I have to think that's a wise decision on his part. There's more to life than just running a business successfully, and he's still relatively young enough to enjoy the years ahead.' He noticed that she had made heavy inroads into the champagne. He stood up. 'I'll get you a top-up, shall I?'

Her hand shook slightly as he filled her glass, then his own. She found herself concentrating absurdly on the dark hairs of his wrist under the heavy links of the gold Rolex watch. The silence grew heavy between them. In desperation Tara decided it was her turn to make conversation. 'You're looking very formal for a weekend. Have you got a business appointment later?'

He shook his head. 'No—er——'

Ah Chee interrupted him. 'Lunch is ready, sir.'

It seemed to Tara that he was relieved, almost as if he had welcomed the interruption.

'Bring your glass with you, Tara!' He stood up with alacrity, ready to usher her into a smaller room that led off the main sitting-room. 'Would you like to—er—wash your hands?' he queried.

'No, I'm fine, thank you,' she responded brightly, by now quite bewildered by the whole set-up. The passionate lover of the night before had disappeared, and in his stead was a sober-suited businessman, a wary expression in his eyes when he looked at her, with the distant formal manners of a stranger.

Lunch was to be served on a small round table covered with a fine white cloth. A single gardenia lay in a shallow bowl as the centrepiece. The china was white porcelain, thin and delicate, with a design of two green dragons chasing each other around the edge. With a mental shrug of her shoulders Tara allowed him to settle her into the chair. If this was a new game he was playing, once more she didn't know the rules.

Ah Chee came to serve her with a bowl of steaming hot soup that smelled delicious, and without warning her tummy rumbled ominously.

'That looks wonderful!' she enthused, but she'd noticed the quick grin on Ryan's face. 'I haven't had any breakfast so I'm starving.'

'Here,' Ryan pushed the bread-basket towards her, 'you sound as if you need that.'

At least he looked and sounded a bit more human, she thought, as she smilingly took a roll. 'I do!' she agreed warmly, breaking it in her hands before buttering a small piece.

Conversation became easier betwen them after

that. It was obvious to her that whatever he wanted to talk about was going to have to wait until lunch was finished. The delicious food helped to break up the awkwardness between them as they started to talk more companionably, but for all that Tara was still aware that Ryan was very much on his guard as far as she was concerned.

Coffee was served in the large sitting-room, and by this time Tara had no inhibitions about kicking off her shoes and curling up in one corner of the big sofa. As Ah Chee left the room to Tara's praise that that had been one of the best meals she had ever had, Ryan told her, 'We won't be disturbed now.' He handed her her coffee, coming to sit next to her, but she was on her guard as she saw the wary, shuttered expression on his face.

'I don't quite know how to say this, but I do know that I owe you a very deep and humble apology.'

'Please, Ryan! This isn't necessary. I told Daddy I understood——'

He interrupted. 'I should have my tongue cut out for what I said to you that day,' he told her roughly. 'My only excuse for over-reacting so much is that I couldn't—no, wouldn't accept that I'd been wrong about you all along. I'm normally pretty good at judging people—but you! Well, I just couldn't make you out. . .' He sighed. 'All the time we were together my instincts were at war. I blamed you for that as well. Tara, I know you haven't wanted to see me these last two weeks, and kissing you last night was a terrible mistake, but can you forgive me?'

She sat absolutely still, incapable of moving a muscle. So, this was what was meant when people spoke of suffering a body blow. She felt numb inside. Kissing her last night had been a mistake, had it? Now he wanted her forgiveness. Well, she didn't feel very forgiving just at this moment, in fact quite the reverse. Slowly the feelings inside her began to unfreeze into a mixture of such pain and anger that she was hard pushed not to scream her agony out loud. Deliberately she put her cup and saucer down on the low table in front of the sofa.

'Tara?'

Hearing her name spoken so gently was the last straw. She stood up.

'You want my forgiveness?' She spoke through gritted teeth. 'Well, let me tell you that you'll never get that even if you live to be a hundred!' She noticed with pleasure his shattered expression. 'I don't know how you even dare ask me for it!' She was well into her stride now, and nothing was going to stop her telling him exactly what she thought of him. 'Of all the arrogant, self-satisfied chauvinist pigs in this world, you have to be worst! I wonder just how many sad, pathetic women have offered you everything, only to have you throw it back in their faces.

'So you made a "terrible mistake" kissing me

last night. Not half as much a mistake as I made by allowing you to do it! Well, this time, boyo, you're going to find out exactly what it feels like to be kicked in the teeth! It'll do you good to be on the receiving-end for a change. You want me in your bed, don't you? You really, really want my body.' She took pleasure from watching him wince. 'Well. . .' She spoke the next words very, very slowly. 'You are never going to get me there. I'm going to be the one castle you don't seize.' The last word ended up in sibilant hiss. She grabbed her bag and fled, ignoring his sudden shout to wait. She slammed the door of his apartment shut almost in his face, and not waiting for the lift ran down the stairs fast and into a providentially waiting taxi, with tears pouring down her cheeks.

CHAPTER NINE

ALTHOUGH Tara had stopped crying by the time she got home it was obvious to all who saw her that something had gone pretty drastically wrong with her day.

'Good God! What on earth's the matter?' Her father had come out of his study just as she entered the house.

'Nothing,' she muttered as she ran past him up the stairs to the sanctuary of her room. The door shut with a slam that reverberated throughout the whole house.

'What's that?' Serena came out of the sitting-room to join her husband, who shrugged his shoulders.

'That was my daughter coming home in a flaming temper.' They eyed each other uneasily.

'Wasn't she going to have lunch with Ryan today?' Serena queried.

'Yes! And the man who's supposed to have quite a way with women of all ages and colours seems to have lost his touch as far as my daughter's concerned,' he finished caustically.

Serena took his arm to lead him back with her into the sitting-room. 'That's because he really cares about her, you see. It's never really mattered to him before. She's rocked him off his feet, but he'll recover.'

'I hope you're right. . .' her husband gave her a quick kiss '. . .because I have an uncomfortable feeling in my bones that Tamara is not going to be at all easy to live with in her present mood!'

Tara lay on her bed in a mood of corroding disillusionment. Her anger had gone, leaving her with the feeling that life wasn't worth living. She couldn't even be bothered to start to tidy up the mess she had left before she went out, but eventually the untidiness began to grate on her nerves. Sighing heavily, she got up and made a start at trying to restore order.

Why had she had the rotten luck to fall in love with a no-good womaniser? Lunch with him had been a total disaster, and he hadn't been a bit like his normal self. 'I bet he was trying to screw up the courage to ask me to marry him,' she told her yellow dress. 'But even gaining control of Hall Bay wasn't enough to make him take the plunge!' she finished viciously, throwing the dress carelessly into the cupboard.

Once her room was tidy Tara was left with nothing to do. There was only one thing that still bugged her, and that was the piece of jade from Brett Moncrieff. If she showed that to her father, then she would also have to give him the note that came with it. Pride had a war with common sense. At least she hadn't been put in a position of refusing an offer of marriage. At this moment in time she wasn't sure if that was a good or bad thing—anyway, it was too valuable a piece to be left just sitting around.

She gave herself a good strong pep-talk before leaving her room. Her father would help her to find a demanding job which required long hours and total dedication, and she would find somewhere to live where there wasn't the slightest possibility of bumping into Ryan. In any case, it was about time she went downstairs to talk about the fabulous party they had given for her. Ever since that disastrous lunch she'd been behaving like a spoilt child, she told herself, and it wasn't fair to take out of her misery on her family.

'Hi!' She walked into her father's study, giving both him and Serena quick kiss. They were watching the end of the news on the TV but her father switched it off as she joined them. She flopped on to the single chair. 'Don't turn it off just because I've come down,' she protested.

'There wasn't anything else worth watching,' her father replied. 'What's that you've got in your hand?'

'Brett Moncrieff sent it to me yesterday.' She handed it over to him. 'He tried to give it to me once before, but I handed it back. I trust you're going to tell me what to do with it. By the way, the party was just the greatest, wasn't it?'

'I hoped you had a good time,' Serena responded.

'I loved every minute, and so did my friends.'

'This is a fantastic piece of jade!' her father enthused, his fingers stroking it admiringly.

'Yes, well, there's also a note that goes with it.' She took it out of her pocket and handed it to him. Her father frowned when he read it, but he didn't immediately give an answer. 'Quite a problem, isn't it?' she said.

'Let me see.' Serena took the little carving into her hands. 'Oh, it's enchanting! You lucky girl, this is a very good piece. You say that Brett Moncrieff gave you this?'

'Yes. It's supposed to be an early wedding present.'

'Oh, dear!' Serena gave her a quick look before putting it down on the table in front of the sofa. 'So you're gong to send it back, then?'

Tara shrugged. 'As no one has asked me to marry them, what other choice do I have?'

'Do you believe this nonsense?' her father asked, tapping the note.

'It's rather difficult. As Ryan hasn't asked me to marry him, I suppose the question's an academic one.'

'Don't be difficult, Tara! Do you believe this to be true?'

Again she shrugged her shoulders before replying, 'I really don't know. . .'

'Does he know about this?' her father asked.

'No, he does not! I don't want you telling him either. He's an arrogant chauvinist pig, and. . .'

Suddenly she broke off in tears. 'I'm sorry,' she choked, 'but he really upset me today. . .'

'Oh, darling!' Serena got up to give her a hug. 'Why don't you tell us what went wrong?'

Tara collapsed into sobs. It took some time before she managed to pull herself together enough to give them some idea of what had happened. 'First of all he tried to apologise; I tried to stop him, but he went on, and then. . . He said it had been a terrible mistake to kiss me last night and would I forgive him! He's always made it clear that he doesn't like or trust me very much. I tried so hard not to fall in love with him.' Her voice faltered. 'He—he made it clear that he wanted me, but nothing else. . . What am I to do?'

'I think you're very tired and should have dinner in bed.' Serena swept her out of the room and back upstairs. 'First, a long hot bath. Then supper. . . After that we'll talk, if you still want to.'

She was as good as her word, abandoning her husband to concentrate totally on Tara, who found it strangely comforting to be cosseted in this way.

When she had finished the last of her supper Serena told her, 'Now I'm going to tell you what I think.' She settled herself more comfortably on the edge of Tara's bed. 'I think Ryan has fallen in love with you. Maybe he doesn't want to admit it to himself, but I think that's the truth.'

Tara allowed the hope she was feeling to show in her face. 'Do you? Do you really think that?'

'I'm fairly sure I'm right. I thought so that day when he brought you home in the taxi. Behaviour like that isn't his style at all! So, OK, he's always had masses of girlfriends. But in all the years I've known him, I've never seen him behave like that to any of them. Hong Kong's a pretty small town, you know, everyone knows everyone else's business. You disturb him—he doesn't know how to handle you. Look how he behaved when he thought you had signed away your shares. He's always been cool and in control, yet where you're concerned he does everything wrong! What was he like when you turned up for lunch today?'

'Very formal, not like himself at all.'

'There you are! I bet he was trying to work up the courage to ask you to marry him.'

'Work up the courage?' Tara looked her astonishment.

'Yes! Don't you see? He isn't at all sure how you feel about him. As far as you're concerned he hasn't exactly behaved well, has he? I guess that people like him who've had great success with women over the years find it hard to express their real, deep feelings when they genuinely fall in love. It's been so easy for him before with all that charm. Now he's met you, and seen that you aren't prepared to fall at his feet, so he doesn't know what to do.'

Tara gave a slow smile. 'I wish I could believe you!'

'I think you know very well that what I'm saying

is the truth. So, you gave him a hard time today; well, there's always tomorrow.'

'What do you mean?' Tara sat up a little straighter on the pillows.

'Why, that it's going to be up to you to arrange the next meeting.'

'I won't do that! I'll not give him the satisfaction of chasing him!'

'OK, OK! Impasse!' Serena smiled. 'Sleep on it. There are ways and ways, you know. . .' She blew her stepdaughter a kiss before leaving her.

Tara spent most of the following week trying to believe what Serena had told her, but the thought that she might be wrong held her back from any positive action. Suppose Ryan wasn't in love with her, what then? And, even if he was, the things she had said to him—well. . . She preferred not to follow that thought through.

She'd had an interview with a firm of stock-brokers with a view to working in their research department, but had found herself being slightly ambivalent about making a definite commitment. In fact, she was being indecisive about virtually everything in her life, she told herself in despair. All she could really think about was Ryan, and how he felt about her.

So, by Friday she came to a momentous decision. She would go round to Ryan's apartment and apologise to him. Further than that, she wasn't prepared to go. Let's take one thing at a time, she told herself firmly.

She was so shaky with nerves when she rang the bell that she felt quite dizzy. Perhaps he wasn't in? Or, worse, maybe he had people with him?

It was Ryan himself who answered the door, looking smoothly non-committal at the sight of her.

She gulped, 'I've come to apologise for what I said to you!'

He stood to one side. 'Come in.'

Tara was torn with indecision. Should she, or shouldn't she? There was very little to help her in his expression.

'Well, I—really that's all. . .' She trailed off miserably.

'At least let me get you a drink.' He shut the door firmly behind her, leading the way towards the big sitting-room. 'Champagne?' he enquired smoothly. 'I seem to remember that you enjoyed it last time you were here.' Was it her imagination or had there been a definite glint in his eyes as he looked at her?

'Thank you.' Nervously she sat down on the edge of an upright chair as he left the room. She listened intently to noises of cupboards being opened and shut before he returned with a tray.

'Now,' he opened the bottle and began to pour the sparkling wine into two glasses, 'what was it you wanted to say to me?' He walked over to hand her a glass. There was no mistaking the sudden amusement in his face.

The swine! He was laughing at her! 'I just came

to say that I was sorry,' she replied stiffly. 'You made me lose my temper.'

'You got cross when I told you kissing you had been a mistake.'

She regarded him with smouldering eyes. 'Yes, I did! No girl would like to be told that.'

'I agree,' he answered smoothly. 'That was a tactical error on my part, and I owe you an apology as well for making it.' He came to stand in front of her, holding her eyes with his own. Nervously, she put her glass down on an adjacent table, not quite sure what to do next, but Ryan had no doubts. He swept her into his arms, and as she opened her mouth to protest he covered it with his.

For a moment she struggled furiously, but the old magic was still as strong as ever, and her body melted in his arms.

'Idiot!' Ryan whispered into her ear. 'Why didn't you guess I was madly in love with you?' His hands, gently stroking, completed her betrayal. 'I'm crazy about you, my beautiful darling. . . Why did you run away?' The warm caressing tones sent delightful shivers down her back.

'I thought you didn't care. . .' she breathed.

He cupped her face in his hands and gave her a lazy smile. 'You thought I didn't care? Crazy girl! I was afraid you didn't love me. It wasn't until you got mad at me after lunch that I dared to hope. Oh, I knew I could make you want me, but that was never going to be enough as far as I was concerned.' His face became serious. 'I've been in love with you almost from the first moment of seeing you at the airport. Oh, I didn't admit it to myself, but it was true. It drove me mad to have you so near me in the office. . . I couldn't think straight while you were around. That's why I told your father I couldn't work with you.' The blue eyes suddenly dimmed a little. 'Do you love me?'

'Yes, I love you! Arrogant, bossy, and far too pleased with yours——' She wasn't allowed to finish as he kissed her again with a sudden fierce urgency. She was weak at the knees by the time he finished.

'If I'd done that last Saturday we wouldn't have wasted a whole week would we?'

'No, I suppose not. . . Why didn't you try to get in touch with me, if you thought I cared?'

He held her closer. 'I was afraid you'd bite my head off again!'

She was indignant at his teasing. 'No, you weren't. Why, I think you guessed I'd come to you!'

He gave a soft laugh before stopping her mouth with kisses until she calmed down.

'I only hoped, I didn't know. . . Anyway, if you hadn't come to see me tonight, then I would have come to find you tomorrow.' His smile was very tender. 'I love you, my darling! I want you around me for the rest of my life. In fact I'm fairly sure I can't live without you. . .' There was no mistaking the passionate sincerity in his voice.

'Is this a proposal?' It was Tara's turn to tease. 'Because, if so, I want you down on your knees!'

He got down on one knee, still holding her hands. 'Will you marry me, my lovely?'

'Sir! This is so sudden!' She gave a little gurgle of laughter as he stood up and swept her into his arms before they collapsed together on to the large sofa.

'Fair maiden! Take pity on this humble servant of yours!' He was holding her tenderly, but his eyes were giving her quite a different message.

Such a wave of love and desire went through her that just for a moment she found it hard to breathe. 'You do me much honour, sir! But this is not a decision to be taken lightly. Oh!' He stopped her mouth with a kiss of such passionate feeling that she lay helpless in his arms, allowing him to plunder the sweetness of her mouth. All coherent thought left her as her senses came alive in rippling waves of pleasure under the warmth of his body.

'Well?' The glinting blue eyes so close to hers were bright with the inner fire of passion.

'Yes, please!' she answered softly, one finger tracing the outline of his mouth.

' "Come live with me, and be my love, and we will all the pleasures prove." ' The beautiful deep voice was full of meaning, and she gave a great sigh of pure satisfaction. 'Now let me give you a quick tour of your future home.' He rolled off the sofa. 'And after that I'll cook you dinner!'

Holding hands, he showed her around the apartment, but he left the large double bedroom till last. 'And this is where I hope you'll spend the night with me.' His eyes were giving her messages that had her feeling weak at the knees again.

'I don't think I'm very hungry. . .for food.' Her voice had been deliberately provocative, and she gave him a tantalising half-smile. She felt the tremor that ran through his body, and slipped a hand through the cotton of his shirt to feel the feverish heat of his skin.

He held her away from him. 'If we get into that bed,' his voice sounded rough, 'I'll make no promises about when I let you leave it!'

She just laughed softly, and pressed her body close to his. He groaned, pulling her even closer, until his mouth found hers.

Somehow he managed to remove most of her clothes without his lips leaving hers. The feel of his hands on her bare skin excited her unbearably as she waited with feverish impatience to feel his nakedness next to hers. The cool white sheets accepted the softness of their bodies.

Ryan lifted himself on one elbow to feast his eyes on the rounded curves so openly displayed. His eyes were now as brilliant as two sapphires as one hand softly stroked and teased the bare flesh. 'You have the most beautiful and erotic body I have ever seen!'

The caressing warmth of his deep voice made her suddenly shy as she pressed herself close to him, feeling the throbbing heat of his manhood leap against her skin.

'I want you so much, my darling,' his voice thickened, 'that I don't think I'll be much good to you this first time, but I promise I'll make it up to you later!'

He took her quickly then, but he was wrong; as she felt him move quickly inside her the wonderful tension built up until she, too, exploded with pleasure at this first joining of their bodies.

She'd always known that he was going to be the most wonderful lover, but he took her to heights that night she'd never dreamed existed. To start with she'd been worried that her inexperience could spoil things for him, but she needn't have been so unsure of herself. Together they embarked on a joyous journey of discovery, learning to please each other with an enthusiasm which it seemed unlikely they would ever lose.

'Do you have to go back and live with your father until we're married?' he teased her the next morning as they lay in bed having a late breakfast. 'Because, if so, we're going to have one of the shortest engagements on record!'

She smiled. 'You can spare me during the day?'

'Only if you promise to be here for lunch!'

She giggled. 'You're impossible!'

'No, just insatiable as far as you're concerned! You're a very lucky girl, you know. . .'

She turned to hit him. 'Just for that remark you're going to have to wait until the evening!'

'You wouldn't be so cruel. . .'

'Maybe I wouldn't, at that. . .' she agreed, giving him a slow smile.

'Oh, God, Tamara! I never thought or dreamt anyone as exciting and beautiful as you existed! It ties me up in knots just to look at you; I can't believe you've promised to marry me.'

'It's just the same for me,' she told him softly. 'I still find it hard to believe that you really love me. It hurt so much when I got that note from Brett. . .'

He grasped her arm, hard. 'What note? What are you talking about?'

'I'm sorry—I forgot you don't know. It was the day of the party. He sent me back the piece of carved jade with a note saying that it was an early wedding present. . .' Her eyes couldn't meet his as she continued a little sadly, 'He said that you had decided to marry me to gain control of Hall Bay. . .'

'Oh, hell!' He slipped out of the bed, grabbing a towel which he caught round his waist, and walked over to the window.

'Ryan?' Tara began to feel a little uncomfortable and frightened. Grabbing his silk dressing-gown, she came to stand behind him, clasping her arms around his waist. 'What is it?'

He gave a great sigh. 'You're always going to remember that, aren't you? It will be there at the back of your mind all the time!'

'No!' Her voice was high with pain. 'If I truly thought that, how could I agree to marry you?'

She hugged him tightly. 'Please, Ryan, don't let that man come between us again.'

He heard the hurt in her voice, and turned to hold her tight in his arms. He kissed her softly on the cheek, but already there were tears in her eyes.

'You don't know what it was like that day at the races. They frightened me!'

He held her closer. 'Don't darling!'

'All the time I was there I was thinking that if only I could get away you would help me.' She sniffed miserably. 'I knew it was my fault, you see. If only I'd told you what I'd done. . . But it was my stupid pride! That morning was the first time I really felt that you believed we were on the same side. . .' Now she was crying in earnest, great, gasping sobs, as he tried to soothe her with whispered endearments. 'When you came to the house I was so happy when I heard your footsteps. . .'

'Ah, dear God! Don't!' She felt the words were wrenched out of some deep well of emotion as his chest rose and fell heavily against hers. 'I can't bear it, Tara!'

'It wasn't your fault, Ryan, it was mine. You weren't to know the truth—how could you have guessed? Daddy told me when we were in Phuket that it had been his idea to keep an eye on me. Anyway, we all know now just who it was who started the whole thing off—my mother. She knew Brett Moncrieff was interested in my shares yet she implied to me that it could be you who was trying to get control of the company. She did everything she could to spoil things for me on my return to Hong Kong. I should have realised sooner that it was she who tried to set me up.' She broke away from his arms, suddenly fierce. 'But if you let her spoil what's between us, then I'll never forgive you! Never!'

He gave an unwilling laugh. 'Come back here, you little hell-cat! Don't you know now that I couldn't leave you even if I wanted to? We've got a lot to learn about each other; everything really except what's on the bottom line, and that's our love for each other. We'll build on that, and build well, because as far as I'm concerned that's a very solid foundation!'

Six weeks later Tara stood by her father, waiting to walk down the aisle of St John's Cathedral on her wedding-day. These last weeks had held surprises, not the least of which was the presence of her mother and stepfather at her wedding.

When Tara had rung her mother with the news that she was engaged, she had expected a volley of verbal abuse. Whether it was a guilty conscience or she had at last decided to let bygones be bygones was anyone's guess, but her mother had been thrilled, and behaved as if nothing had happened between them.

She had insisted that her daughter return to have her wedding dress made in London, yet had seemed quite content to let her ex-husband and his new wife arrange the wedding reception in Hong Kong. She'd made it perfectly clear that she had no intention of being left out of anything, and had done her best to charm Ryan.

He had insisted on accompanying his future wife back to England, and they had had a frantically busy ten days meeting his relations as well as hers. When her mother was at her most charming it had always been difficult to resist her, and Tara was so happy now that she didn't really try. She was just tremendously grateful that her happy time was not going to be spoilt by a family feud.

So here Patricia Chacewater was, waiting for her only daughter to appear, dressed in such a stunning outfit that it was quite obvious she intended to outshine everyone.

Marcel Chang, although not in the church, had contrived to send Tara a present of such overpowering opulence on the announcement of her engagement that it was clearly a peace-offering. It had been sent with a letter that cleverly set him out as the innocent dupe of Brett Moncrieff, so that to refuse to believe him would be churlish. Even her father had agreed that he had lost enough face over the whole business, so he decided that his daughter should accept the present gratefully.

As the music began to swell in a triumphant burst of sound, Tara's father bent his head to whisper, 'All right, my darling? Shall we go?'

She nodded her head, giving him a quick smile, but really all her thoughts were centred on the man standing waiting for her at the end of the long aisle.

HARLEQUIN ✦ PRESENTS®

BARBARY WHARF

Home to the *Sentinel*
Home to passion, heartache and love

Charlotte Lamb

The BARBARY WHARF six-book saga continues with
Book Two, BATTLE FOR POSSESSION. Daniel Bruneille
is the head of the *Sentinel*'s Foreign Affairs desk and Roz
Amery is a foreign correspondent. He's bossy and
dictatorial. She's fiercely ambitious and independent.
When they clash it's a battle—a battle for possession!

And don't forget media tycoon Nick Caspian and his
adversary Gina Tyrrell. Will Gina survive the treachery of
Nick's betrayal and the passion of his kiss...?

BATTLE FOR POSSESSION (Harlequin Presents #1509)
available in November.

HARLEQUIN ROMANCE®

Valerie Bloomfield comes home to Orchard Valley, Oregon, for the saddest of reasons. Her father has suffered a serious heart attack, and now his three daughters are gathering at his side, praying he'll survive.

Orchard Valley

This visit home will change Valerie's life—especially when she meets Colby Winston, her father's handsome and strong-willed doctor!

"The Orchard Valley trilogy features three delightful, spirited sisters and a trio of equally fascinating men. The stories are rich with the romance, warmth of heart and humor readers expect, and invariably receive, from Debbie Macomber."

—Linda Lael Miller

Don't miss the Orchard Valley trilogy by Debbie Macomber:

VALERIE   Harlequin Romance #3232 (November 1992)
STEPHANIE   Harlequin Romance #3239 (December 1992)
NORAH   Harlequin Romance #3244 (January 1993)

Look for the special cover flash on each book!

Available wherever Harlequin books are sold   ORC-G

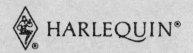

HARLEQUIN®

THE TAGGARTS OF TEXAS!

Harlequin's Ruth Jean Dale brings you
THE TAGGARTS OF TEXAS!

Those Taggart men—strong, sexy and hard to resist...

You've met Jesse James Taggart in FIREWORKS!
Harlequin Romance #3205 (July 1992)

Now meet Trey Smith—he's THE RED-BLOODED YANKEE!
Harlequin Temptation #413 (October 1992)

Then there's Daniel Boone Taggart in SHOWDOWN!
Harlequin Romance #3242 (January 1993)

And finally the Taggarts who started it all—in LEGEND!
Harlequin Historical #168 (April 1993)

Read all the Taggart romances!
Meet all the Taggart men!

Available wherever Harlequin books are sold.

HARLEQUIN ROMANCE®

Harlequin Romance
invites you to a
celebrity wedding—or is it?

Find out in Bethany Campbell's
ONLY MAKE-BELIEVE (#3230),
the November title in

THE BRIDAL COLLECTION

THE BRIDE was pretending.
THE GROOM was, too.
BUT THE WEDDING was real—the second time!

Available this month (October)
in The Bridal Collection
TO LOVE AND PROTECT
by Kate Denton
Harlequin Romance #3223

Wherever Harlequin Books are sold.